Cindy, meet

The thing about staring at your shoes while you're walking is that you're unable to see where you're going, which means if, say, there's a bank of water fountains in your path, you end up bumping into them. And if your book bag isn't zippered like, say, mine never is, it'll probably go sailing across the hall and everything will fall out of it. Including any maxi pads you may have stashed in there.

"Are you, uh, okay?" a voice asked as I tried to pick myself up off the floor. Along with the book bag, I, too, had gone sailing across the hall.

I prayed that somehow, in the few moments between the water fountain and my fall, Adam Silver had left the hallway and that the husky voice belonged to someone who had just transferred to Castle Heights that morning and therefore hadn't yet been briefed on my avoid-at-all-cost status. But when I looked up and into those brown eyes that I now saw weren't just brown, but also had cool flecks of gold in them, I realized that I had the starring role in the latest Hollywood blockbuster horror movie.

"Yeah, I'm fine," I mumbled, scrambling to pick up the maxi pads, sitting there right next to his scuffed Pumas.

"Are you sure? That was a pretty gnarly wipeout."

Oh my God. That voice . . . it was better in person than it had ever sounded in my daydreams.

"Happens all the time," I said as I scooped up the Kotex. "See, I'm fine," I said as I stood up and winced, wondering whether I had broken my tailbone. I looked up at him. Now was my chance to say something—anything—to make an impression on him, because God knows I'd never have the chance again. I took a deep breath and summoned up all my courage.

"Bye," I said as I limped off.

OTHER BOOKS YOU MAY ENJOY

Cindy Ella

ROBIN PALMER

speak
An Imprint of Penguin Group (USA) Inc.

SPEAK

Published by the Penguin Group

Penguin Group (USA) Inc., 345 Hudson Street, New York, New York 10014, U.S.A.

Penguin Group (Canada), 90 Eglinton Avenue East, Suite 700, Toronto,
Ontario M4P 2Y3 Canada (a division of Pearson Penguin Canada Inc.)

Penguin Books Ltd, 80 Strand, London WC2R 0RL, England

Penguin Group Ireland, 25 St Stephen's Green, Dublin 2, Ireland
(a division of Penguin Books Ltd)

Penguin Group (Australia), 250 Camberwell Road, Camberwell, Victoria 3124, Australia
(a division of Pearson Australia Group Pty. Ltd)

Penguin Books India Pvt. Ltd., 11 Community Centre,
Panchsheel Park, New Delhi - 110 017, India

Penguin Group (NZ), 67 Apollo Drive, Rosedale, North Shore 0632, New Zealand
(a division of Pearson New Zealand Ltd)

Penguin Books (South Africa) (Pty) Ltd, 24 Sturdee Avenue,
Rosebank, Johannesburg 2196, South Africa

Registered Offices: Penguin Books Ltd, 80 Strand, London WC2R 0RL, England

Published by Speak, an imprint of Penguin Group (USA) Inc., 2008

1   3   5   7   9   10   8   6   4   2

CIP Data is available
SPEAK ISBN 978-0-14-240392-1

Printed in the United States of America

In memory of my mother,

Ursula Boes Palmer

Ich liebe Dich

Acknowledgments

With utmost eternal gratitude to Cindy's two fairy god-mothers—

My incredible editor, Jennifer Bonnell—whose talent, enthusiasm, warmth, and humor have spoiled me forever. Thanks for supplying such a happy ending—for both Cindy *and* myself.

Agent *extraordinaire* Kate Lee—whose belief in me and tireless efforts on my behalf mean the world to me. Thanks for not only doing your best for me, but for always pushing me to do mine as well. I couldn't be in better hands.

Special thanks to Maggie Dintaman, Jordan Roter, Shira Hoffman, and Rachel Waxman for their invaluable feedback on various drafts of the manuscript. And special, *special* thanks to Cynthia Greenburg for hers.

And, lastly, to everyone who let me borrow their faith in me on the days when mine was M.I.A. because I was too busy worrying about whether I hadn't completely lost my mind when I made the decision to trade in my expense account and Manolo Blahniks so I could spend my days alone in a room writing—especially my family, Marilyn R. Atlas, Christina Beck, Julie Bradberry, Laura Clark, Nicole Dintaman, Maureen Foley, Julie Golden, Veronica Goodchild, Linda Sheldon, Chad Hoffman, Kellie Keane, Amy Loubalu, Sara Mornell, Laila Nabulsi, the real Michael Rosenberg, Rene Smallwood, Zoya Spivakovsky, and Terri Wagener.

prologue

To the Editor:

For the two years that I've been a student at Castle Heights, I've been a very loyal reader of the *Courier,* your so-called newspaper, even though you have refused to print any of my letters. However, I thought you should know that as of today, you can no longer count me as a reader. Let me put it this way: if people needed a subscription to get your so-called newspaper instead of picking it up for free outside of the cafeteria, I'd be canceling mine.

The reason for this letter is that I was positively DISGUSTED by your most recent issue and the way that EVERY SINGLE article in it was about the upcoming prom. As if that's the ONLY thing that is happening in this world. If you bothered to turn on the news once in a while, or picked up a REAL newspaper, you'd see that the world is bigger than this dumb private school and that trying to fight global warming or find a cure for cancer is a little more important than "The Best Nail Salons to Go to for a Preprom Manicure Where You Won't Get An Infection." You know, not EVERYONE in this school is going to the prom, so how do you think those of us who aren't going feel when we pick up our school newspaper expecting to be brought up-to-date about what's going on in the world and instead all we find is "The Best Diets to Lose Those Ten Preprom Pounds in One Week"???

As far as I'm concerned, this last issue of the *Courier* is the straw that broke the camel's back, because it shows just how superficial everyone at this school is. All anyone is interested in is wearing the right jeans, and what the hippest purse is, and how to get ahold of that necklace that Lindsay Lohan was wearing in last week's *Us Weekly*. When you print articles like this, you're just adding to the problem. This is a school full of label-obsessed kids who just want to be carbon copies of everyone else. And the problem with this society is that the stupid PROM has become the be-all, end-all of the high school experience. Like if you don't go it somehow means that you're defective. YEAH, RIGHT. So you have a school full of kids who spend their nights not sleeping because they're worried that they're not going to be asked, or they're worrying who to ask so that they seem cool. Again, I say YEAH, RIGHT. If those kids spent five of those minutes thinking about how to better the world rather than how to become more popular because they had the right dress or the right date, then we'd solve all our problems in no time.

Don't you people realize that the prom is just part of all of that fairy-tale stuff we were fed when we were kids? Sure, maybe once upon a time it had some meaning—as a rite of passage to early adulthood—but those days are over. Now it's just all about big business. And if all of you girls out there think that some prince is going to show up in a limo and sweep you off your feet and you'll live a happily-ever-after pimple-free life, I have two words for you: AS IF!

All you're doing is adding to what I call the "Noah's Ark Syndrome" or "You Complete Me Syndrome" (à la *Jerry Maguire*), which is the idea that a person is only half a person unless they have a mate or, in this case, a prom date. Just because a person doesn't have a prom date doesn't mean there's something wrong with her. Maybe it just means she's picky and/or not afraid to be alone until the right person comes along. Look at George Clooney: he's always talking about how he'll never get married again and I doubt anyone would consider HIM a loser.

By making the prom out to be the end-all, be-all of the whole high school experience, you're seriously hurting the feelings of those students who might want to go but haven't been asked, therefore making them feel even MORE unpopular, which is not only mean but will also give you bad karma. The prom is just another stupid way to divide the students of the school into "popular" and "nonpopular." Did we not learn anything from all those PSAs on Must See TV about how important it is for everyone to unite, no matter what their color, sexual orientation, or social standing? I know I'm only a sophomore, so I couldn't go to the prom unless I was asked by a junior or senior, but even if I WERE asked, I wouldn't go.

I know I'm not alone here in thinking that you should be ashamed of yourselves.

Sincerely,
Cindy E. Gold

If the hostile hush that fell over the Castle Heights High lunchroom when I walked out of the cafeteria bay with my tuna-fish sandwich the day the letter appeared was any indication, it was pretty clear that I *was* alone in my thoughts.

It was the Thursday after Memorial Day and the entire day had been a walking nightmare: snickers, whispers, conversations that ground to a halt whenever I entered the room. The kind of stuff that really pumps up a fifteen-and-a-half-year-old girl's self-esteem. As you can imagine, with the name Cindy Ella Gold, I was used to a fair amount of teasing, but nothing like what I experienced that day.

There I was thinking I was being of service to my fellow nonpopular/nonpromgoing classmates by being the official "We're Not Going to Take It" poster girl, but instead of gratitude and respect, all I got were dirty looks and a schoolwide silent treatment. Even the weirdest kids in school—like Eliza Nesbit, who wore reindeer sweaters all winter, and Maury Scheinberg, who spoke in video-game-speak instead of English—wouldn't look me in the eye. Within the course of a few hours, I had gone from being just another average kid to the most untouchable Untouchable of Castle Heights High.

"Why'd *this* have to be the letter they finally printed?" I moaned to my two BFFs, India and Malcolm, as we sat under our bougainvillea tree that day eating our lunches. The smell of clove cigarettes wafted over from a group of girls dressed in black who were taking turns reading their Sylvia Plath–lite journal entries aloud. "Why couldn't they have printed the one about how the cafeteria should be demolished so no one has to go through the awful experience of figuring out where to sit?"

"You don't think you'll have to be homeschooled now, do you?" asked Malcolm.

I ignored him. He could be such a drama queen at times. "I mean, I knew what I wrote would piss the popular kids off," I said as I took a bite of my sandwich and watched a big glop of tuna fall onto my brand-new CULTURAL ICON

5

IN TRAINING T-shirt. "But I honestly thought everyone else would be thrilled that someone was finally taking a stand about how the prom is just one more attempt by the establishment to keep us down."

"What are you talking about?" Malcolm stopped his lunchtime ritual of inspecting his khakis for the tiniest speck of dirt and looked up, sighing as his eyes zeroed in on my latest attempt to accessorize with tuna.

"You know, how the prom separates the haves from the have-nots; the popular from the unpopular—" I stopped, as Malcolm started frantically rubbing at the blossoming stain on my nonexistent boobs.

"Those who take deep full breaths from their core instead of quick shallow ones," finished India, whose parents owned a chain of yoga studios in town called Blissed Out. "Cin, you spoke the truth—but unfortunately it's one of those dirty little truths that people don't like to think about. They'd rather remain ignorant than search within for answers." She stood up and stretched before settling into a down-dog pose. "A tree doesn't grow branches with water alone, right?" she said. With her long blond hair covering her face, she looked like a supergorgeous version of Cousin It from *The Addams Family.*

Malcolm and I looked at each other, baffled. "Huh?" we said. Even though I've known India for years, and even worked part-time at one of the studios on Sundays, and was therefore used to hearing this kind of Zen mumbo jumbo on a regular basis, it still tended to go over my head.

"Never mind." India sighed from behind her hair.

"Look, what it comes down to is that no one who's unpopular wants to be reminded of that," said Malcolm. "They want to believe that if they just hold on long enough, they, too, can pull a Farmer Ted." Farmer Ted was the character that Anthony Michael Hall played in *Sixteen Candles* who went from geekness to greatness in ninety-one minutes. Malcolm processed everything in life by comparing it to eighties movies. Ms. Highland, our guidance counselor, was convinced it was some sort of personality disorder.

India rejoined us on the ground. "Hey, Wally, I'm so with you in spirit!" she yelled out to Wally Twersky, Castle Heights's resident tree hugger, as he strummed "We Shall Overcome" on his guitar for the tenth straight lunch period as part of his protest against the fact that the school had uprooted endangered trees from across the country and replanted them here in an attempt to spruce up the campus grounds. She patted me on the knee. "I'm sure it'll all blow over by Monday," said India. "Especially after Danny Miller's party this weekend. And *especially* since Jessica Rokosny just got out of rehab."

Malcolm let out a relieved sigh and started inspecting his loafers for scuffs. "Brilliant. With Jessica back, you'll definitely be in the clear." Not only was Jessica a self-taught "pharmacist," she was also the senior-class slut, so the chances of her doing something outrageous to take the focus off of me were pretty good.

"I guess," I said glumly.

"Hey, no matter what happens—you know, if you do end up having to leave school because the teasing gets so bad or what not—you'll always have us," he promised.

Malcolm was right. I *did* have them, and for that I was very grateful. I had met India on the first day of fifth grade when I moved to L.A. from New Jersey, and Malcolm, on our first day at Castle Heights. Malcolm lives in South-Central L.A., so he has to take three buses every day just so he can go to our school, which is supposed to be one of the best in the city, although I have no idea who exactly decides those things. So that they wouldn't be accused of being too elitist, Castle Heights gave out scholarships to underprivileged youth and Malcolm was one of them, even though you'd never be able to tell by looking at his wardrobe and iPod library. But I don't feel sorry for him, because while he may be one of my best friends, he can also be a total diva. He puts La Lohan to shame at times. However, I tend to cut him some slack when he starts to have a meltdown. Finding yourself in a predominantly white private high school after growing up in the 'hood is enough to cause anyone some angst.

The three of us made up what we called the Outsiders' Insider Club. Malcolm's black and gay, so it's pretty obvious why he's an outsider. And India—well, even though we live in L.A., where there's a lot of boho-lite going on, people aren't all that tolerant when it comes to the old-school hippies like India who follow strict hundred percent vegan diets and don't shave their armpits.

And me? In a way I'm even more of an outsider because I'm just normal. I'm not gay and I'm not a hippy. I'm not ugly and I'm not beautiful. I'm thin (more like scrawny), but I have no muscle tone. I'm not remedial-math-class dumb, but I'm not egghead brilliant.

I'm just . . . *average*. At least by L.A. standards. Now, if I lived someplace like Twin Falls, Idaho, maybe I'd be considered kind of special. But here in L.A., where everyone's a size two, looks like an Abercrombie model, and has been on the road to Harvard since preschool? Forget it. At least Malcolm and India are dramatically different. But for me, the normal one who kind of blends into the crowd, growing up in L.A. can be hard. Because here, "normal" equals "invisible."

But that Wednesday I sure wasn't invisible. As I skulked down the hall after lunch, trying to tune out the snickers and whispers that had become the sound track to my life, I prayed that Jessica Rokosny hadn't completely cleaned up her act in rehab. *Are You there, God? It's me, Cindy,* I thought as I wiped off the "Cindy Ella's just pissed 'cuz she's a freak and no one will EVER ask her to prom" graffiti that someone had scrawled on my locker during lunch. *Listen, I'm cool with You keeping Jessica clean and sober,* I thought,

*but can You make it so that she ends up making out with at
least one inappropriate guy or girl at Danny Miller's party this
Saturday so that people will be talking about that on Monday
and not me?*

I didn't know where I stood on the God thing, and
whether I was just wasting my time asking for divine
intervention, but I did know that it sucked being a non-
prom girl in an all-prom world.

chapter one

B.T.L. (Before The Letter) I always thought that major life-altering moments happened in dramatic settings. Like New Orleans during Hurricane Katrina, or Bali during a tsunami, or when Ross rushed to the airport to try to stop Rachel from moving to Paris on the series finale of *Friends*. So the fact that mine took place in my bedroom on the Tuesday night after Memorial Day was kind of a letdown.

Not only did Memorial Day mean people all over the world could begin to wear white pants again, but it also meant that prom mania got amped up about a hundred notches. All you had to do was pick up a copy of *Seventeen* or *Teen Vogue* to see that it had overtaken the entire country, but in L.A., it was *really* bad. Especially at Castle Heights. And especially if you were the twins, a.k.a the Clones, a.k.a Ashley and Britney, a.k.a. my stepsisters. Because they were seniors, they had only one last chance to take part in this rite of passage.

Case in point: the conversation at dinner that night at Casa de Gold.

Even though it was supposed to be a "family dinner," my dad, as the head of the legal division at a major film studio where the unofficial motto was "If you don't come in on Saturday, don't bother coming in on Sunday," was working late. So that night, without him there to tell us about whom he had slapped with multimillion-dollar lawsuits that day, the topic of conversation was, yet again, the prom. Just like it had been every day and night for the last three weeks.

"I think it's, like, *totally* bogus that Dylan Schoenfield got a Jaden without telling us first," announced Ashley that evening, spearing a piece of broccoli, as we sat at the dining-room table. Ashley was on her "Green Foods Only" diet that week as opposed to her "Orange Foods Only" diet (carrots and orange Gatorade) or her "Red Foods Only" diet (beets and cherry Life Savers).

I moved around in my chair, trying to get comfortable. Clarissa, my stepmother, and her decorator had settled on a Zen monastery look for the house, so the furnishings were sparse and uncomfortable. When my dad and Clarissa decided to pull a Brady Bunch, she convinced him that the family would have a better chance at bonding if we moved into a different house, even though our house on Norton was big enough for the five of us (soon to be six, once she got pregnant with my half brother, Spencer). They ended up buying another Tudor three blocks away from our old one before knocking it down ("bad vibes," said the house psychic that Clarissa's decorator had brought in) and building a massive brown contemporary. Seeing that we lived in Hancock Park, which is an area that's very New England–looking with its Tudors and brick, it stuck out like a sore thumb.

"Yeah, especially since she was *supposed* to be our best friend," agreed Britney, as she reached for a piece of bread. Unlike Ashley, Britney was on an intimate basis with carbs. However, like Ashley, she was just as thin. Since the seriousness of slander and defamation of character had been drilled into me by my dad since the time I could walk, I'd never go as far to suggest that Brit kept her weight down with a little help (i.e. her finger down her throat). That being said, I would have done anything to have just a quarter of their boobage and butts. Instead I look like a flat-chested, curveless, bony-butted twelve-year-old boy.

Ashley and Britney weren't identical twins—Ashley was 5' 2" and blond, while Britney was 5' 7" and brunette—but they both looked like extras on *The O.C.* As did their pod of friends, which is how India came up with the "Clones" nickname. They all dressed the same (whatever pair of jeans and trendy top that was deemed cool that month by *Lucky* magazine), and they all had the same haircut (whatever Cameron Diaz was flaunting in the most recent

In Style). Just look at their names: Ashley and Britney. Could you *get* more early-nineties generic?

"Mom, we need Jadens, too. Can you please call her and see if she'll make us some?" begged Ashley.

Jaden, an ex-heroin addict/teenage runaway/hooker, had recently become the patron designer saint of all the young female actresses and pop stars and therefore a celebrity in her own right. Clarissa had briefly sponsored her when they were both in AA but hadn't talked to her in years.

"Sweetie, the prom's only three weeks away! And I just read that she's going to be making all of Madonna's costumes for her next tour," said Clarissa as she tried to get Spencer to eat some barebecue tofu from the Whole Foods deli counter. Like me, he was having none of it. Spencer and I were two of the only people in L.A. who preferred actual meat to soy-based products. I kept "accidentally" dropping mine on the floor in hopes that Sushi, our beagle, would eat it, but he wasn't interested, either.

"Mom, pleasepleaseplease," said Britney. "Don't you want us to have a shot at winning Best Dress?" At Castle Heights, there wasn't just Prom Queen and King. There was Best Dress, Best Shoes, Best Accessories, and Best Hair.

Clarissa sighed and smoothed her already sleek blond bob. People were always saying she looked like a blond Anna Wintour, the editor of *Vogue*. "I guess I could call her and remind her that I was the one who heard her fifth step . . ."

According to an old TV movie I had seen on Oxygen a few weeks before, the fifth step in twelve-step programs is when you tell someone all your worst secrets so you won't drink again.

"Isn't that, like, *blackmail*?" I piped up as I twisted my frizzy blond curls into a makeshift bun so they'd stop dipping into the barbecue sauce on my plate.

The three of them turned, surprised to see me sitting there. Because I wasn't going to the prom, I had ceased to exist in their orbit over the last few weeks, which, frankly, was fine with me. It saved me from having to suffer through the Clones' running commentary on my shortcomings, i.e., my lack of fashion sense ("Tan Uggs are *so* five minutes ago—if you have to wear them, at least get them in, like, pink or baby blue"), my taste in music ("Avril Lavigne is *so* emo whiny vagina"), and my grooming habits ("not waxing your eyebrows is *so* 1970s"). Even though they swore their "constructive criticism" was because they wanted me to be able to experience what it felt like to be popular like they were, I didn't buy it. I think it was a way for them to work out the resentment they had toward Clarissa for trading in her first two husbands for better models after a few years. At least that's what my shrink, Dr. Greenburg, once said.

"Of course not, sugar," replied Clarissa, giving up on

the tofu and letting Spencer do what he really wanted, which was to gnaw on the pepper mill. Upon hearing the word *sugar*, Spencer started kicking his legs. Even though he was only a year old, he already had two great loves in life: eating as much sugar as possible, and being naked, both of which he tried to do as often as he could. "I'm just . . . reminding her of the good old times. And how, with her career going the way it is, I'd hate for the press to find out that she slept with a certain married action-adventure star for money when she was underage, so I want to do everything I can to protect her. So, you see, it's actually the *opposite* of blackmail—it's an old friend looking out for her!" Clarissa may have grown up in a trailer park on a Louisiana bayou and dropped out of high school when she got pregnant with the Clones at sixteen, but she wasn't stupid. My dad always said she would've made a great defense attorney or studio exec.

"Sure sounds like blackmail to me," I said under my breath as I dropped another piece of tofu on the floor for Sushi, who took one sniff before going back to compulsively licking himself.

Clarissa put on her "concerned" look (which, thanks to her Botox addiction, wasn't much different from her "annoyed," "amused," or "bored" looks) and leaned toward me. "Cindy Ella, is something the matter? You've been very short-tempered lately." She grabbed my arm and started rolling up the sleeve of my hoodie. "Can I see your arms, please?" Ever since she had caught the tail end of last month's Lifetime Original Movie about cutting, Clarissa was petrified that I might start self-mutilating just because I had actual moods and wasn't on antidepressants like her and the Clones.

Clarissa likes to call me by my "given name" because she finds it "just darling." I find it mortifying. The "Ella" is for Ella Fitzgerald, who was my mom's favorite singer, but of course everyone thinks I'm named after the fairy tale character. The irony is that I absolutely hate fairy tales. I think the way they portray girls as helpless damsels in distress who need to be rescued by princes in order to live happily ever after sends a very damaging message to today's youth. Well, at least that's what Gloria Steinem, the grandmother of feminism, said in a documentary I once saw on the History Channel as I was flipping to catch *The Hills* on MTV.

"She's fine," said Ashley as she speared a pickle. "She's just upset because she feels left out seeing that we're busy with the prom and can't spend as much quality time with her."

Maybe it's just me, but I don't consider bullying me into writing their English papers or forcing me into a game of "Does This Make Me Look Fat?" (where they try on every outfit in their closet and then parade in front of me saying "Okay, how about from *this* angle?") "quality time."

"Or maybe it's because the prom reminds her that

other than that dweeb Michael Rosenberg, she's never even been on a date before," added Britney as she reached for another piece of bread, ignoring Clarissa's look of disapproval.

Britney wasn't wrong—both about Michael Rosenberg being a dweeb *and* my only date so far. Our dads play golf together and last summer Clarissa dragged me with them to a barbecue at the Rosenbergs' house in hopes that he and I would hit it off. I guess he was cute enough if you go for the pudgy Jewish wannabe rapper type (which I didn't), but the fact that he started every sentence with "yo, check this" and spent the entire afternoon responding to e-mails on his Sidekick was a major turnoff. When he wasn't e-mailing he was busy talking about himself, so you can imagine my surprise when I got an e-mail from him the next day asking me if I wanted to go to the New Beverly to see a *Fast Times at Ridgemont High/Say Anything* double feature. Even though those are two of my favorite movies, I didn't want to go with *him,* but because Clarissa said she'd give me twenty-five bucks if I went, I did.

I deserved more like *fifty* it was so horrible. First of all, he made me pay for my own ticket (yes, I'm a feminist, but I'm what they call a nouveau one, which means that part of my mission is to help guys feel empowered again) and second of all, he spent the entire night talking with his mouth full of popcorn about the stupid movie business.

Needless to say I wasn't into him, and gauging from

the fact that I never heard from him again, it wasn't like he was into me, either.

"Michael Rosenberg," said Clarissa as she tapped her French manicured nail on the table. "Michael Rosenberg . . . he's a junior this year at Buckley, isn't he?"

"Yeah . . . so?" I replied warily as I moved the tofu around on my plate.

"Well, sugar, that means he's got a *prom!*" Clarissa trilled as she flashed her just-bleached smile.

As soon as she said "sugar," Spencer looked up from trying to unsnap his onesie and gurgled.

"So?" I said even more warily.

"Maybe I should call Mrs. Rosenberg and see who he's taking," she mused.

"Uh-uh—no thanks," I said firmly.

"Excellent," Ashley said as she high-fived Britney.

"Clarissa, please don't do that," I pleaded.

"Why not? He's absolutely darlin'! I never did understand why you two never went out a second time."

"Well, other than the fact that he never called me again, even if he *had* I would've had to say no if only because he had no idea *Lord of the Rings* was based on a book," I replied.

She pushed her plate out of the way and lit a cigarette. In Clarissaland, food outside of the kitchen is a crime punishable by death ("I've told you about my childhood fear of ants, Cindy Ella"), but smoking while people are still eating is fine.

"Cindy Ella, honey, you're going to get yourself into a lot of trouble if you don't lower your standards a bit. You don't want to end up old and alone like your aunt Rhoda, do you?" she asked as she exhaled.

Rhoda was my dad's sister and the only decent female role model I had. Yes, she was single, but she was a senior producer for CNN, which meant that she was flying around the world covering wars, so second dates were hard to schedule. And in this case, "old" was thirty-seven.

"She's right, Cindy," said Ashley. "Plus I heard that you only end up burning like sixty calories an hour reading or watching TV. That's, like, *nothing*."

"Well, I can't imagine you burn that much more working your Sidekick, which is what Michael spends all his time doing," I retorted.

"Mom's right," said Britney. "If he doesn't have a date already, you should go with him. That way you'll show them."

"Show who what?"

"The kids at school. That you're not a lesbian," she said calmly, reaching for another piece of bread before Clarissa yanked the breadbasket out of the way.

"What?! Why would people think I'm a lesbian?"

Ashley rolled her eyes. "Because you're always talking about how you think the prom's dumb and you'd have no interest in going even if you were asked."

"And you could get a T-shirt made up that says FYI—I

AM GOING TO THE PROM. JUST NOT THIS ONE," said Britney. "If you want, I could help you bedazzle it."

"Let me get this straight," I said. "Just because I don't see the point in spending a Friday night wearing some ridiculously overpriced dress and painfully pointy shoes, eating bad salmon, and slow-dancing with some boy who has sweaty palms, I'm a *lesbian*?" I asked.

"You know, honey, I keep meaning to tell you that Dr. Gerstein and I have decided that even if you were a lesbian, your daddy and I would be okay with it," said Clarissa as she dumped the bread in the garbage. Dr. Gerstein was Clarissa's shrink. "Just like Jane's parents finally were."

"Who's Jane?" I asked.

"The girl in one of the Lifetime movies," she replied. "Now, I can't say it would be my *first* choice for how you lived your life, but I'd find a way to eventually accept it. Otherwise you might start cutting yourself, which would be a shame because your olive skin is one of your best attributes."

"I so can't believe this," I said under my breath as I searched the table for something edible that wasn't green or tofu-based.

Ashley pushed away her plate and sighed. "Brit and I were talking about it on the way home today and we really think it's time for an attitude invention here."

"You mean an 'intervention'?" I asked.

"That's what I said. So, like, why do you insist on being so negative about the prom?"

"It's just that it has no meaning," I replied. "It's supposed to be a rite of passage, but it's not. It's so . . . superficial."

"So? What's wrong with superficial?" asked Britney.

The three of them stared at me, patiently waiting for an answer.

The sad thing is that they really *are* that clueless, so even if I tried to continue the conversation it would be like trying to communicate with Martians from Planet Juicy Couture. "Nothing." I sighed. "Can I be excused?"

"No, sugar. The girls are in the middle of trying to bond with you." According to Dr. Greenburg, bonding is hard to do in blended families. Especially in blended families that see nothing wrong with superficiality.

It was Dr. Greenburg that I had to thank for my dad and Clarissa hooking up. After my mom died and we moved to L.A. from New Jersey, my dad put me in therapy for my twelfth birthday. I had been telling him that all my new friends went and I guess he wanted me to feel like I fit in. Dr. Greenburg is the "Greenburg" in Gerstein Greenburg Gugliotta and Associates. It sounds like a law firm, but it's a "wellness center for family issues." One afternoon in the reception area, as my dad was waiting for me to finish, he met Clarissa, who was waiting for the Clones to be done with Dr. Golden and Dr. Gugliotta. They started dating, and within a month we were just one more party of five waiting for a table at Twin Dragon on Sunday nights so that we could chow down on kung pao chicken and egg rolls—which I now know Clarissa was only doing to impress my dad, because once they got engaged she became the health-food police. We're not even allowed to order egg rolls now. Nothing fried. Instead, we have to get those rubbery Vietnamese spring rolls, which is like eating eyeballs.

"You see, Cindy," Ashley went on. "You have to remember: we're related by marriage here. So when you act like this? It's, like, a *total* reflection on us."

"Which is so not okay," added Britney.

I could see that trying to defend myself was useless. "Okay, fine. I get it. I promise I'll change my attitude. *Now* can I be excused?" I asked again.

This time I didn't wait for a response. I just gave Spencer a kiss on the forehead and got up and walked away.

Not that a response ever came. They were already back on the subject of Jaden by the time I made it to the stairs.

chapter two

When I'm feeling lonely and misunderstood, there are only three things that can cheer me up: a good eighties movie; Ben & Jerry's Chunky Monkey; or a *Sex and the City* episode. It's a good thing that *Sex and the City* is in syndication and can be found almost every hour on the hour, because after that dinner I needed at least two episodes to recover. Chunky Monkey was a nonoption thanks to the lack of a freezer in my bedroom (I certainly wasn't risking going downstairs for another round of Pin the Loser Tail on Cindy), but I did have a Toblerone bar in my book bag.

I love my bedroom, which is a good thing, seeing that I spend so much time there. Even though the decorator said the red-and-green Ralph Lauren look ruined the feng shui, Clarissa had let us decorate our bedrooms how we wanted, so she couldn't complain. Mine has the standard teenage girl stuff: TV, desk, computer, bookcase, iPod speakers, red velvet chaise lounge. I guess that part isn't so standard. Malcolm, India, and I had found the chaise at the Fairfax High flea market one Sunday and I fell in love with it. Clarissa was sure that it was infested with fleas or lice, but I refused to throw it away.

I was lying on the chaise with my jeans unbuttoned (tofu always made me bloat), wondering if I was indeed the loser that the Clones thought I was and flipping through channels to catch Carrie and friends, when I came upon Larry King interviewing Naomi Wolf on CNN. I'm not a big Larry fan (I much prefer Anderson Cooper—not only is he a hottie, he's supercompassionate), so I don't know what made me stop flipping, but I did. I guess it was what my friend Phoolendu at the yoga studio would call "kismet." That's like fate, but much more dramatic.

I may be a nouveau feminist, but I'm embarrassed to say I had never heard of Naomi. When I Googled her, I found out she had been famous back in the nineties for writing this book called *The Beauty Myth,* which was about how the cosmetic industry set these ridiculous beauty standards for women to live up to that only maybe three supermodels in the world would ever be able to achieve. I haven't read it, but *The New York Times* called it one of the most important books of the twentieth century, so you just know it has to be good.

Anyway, after Naomi finished slamming a certain Academy Award–winning actress who is known for overdoing the Botox to the point where she's unable to show any expression, she started talking about how the pressure for women to look good started way early in life, like all the way back to the prom. Then she went on a rant about how the prom was to *Seventeen* like Valentine's Day was to Hallmark—just another way for the fashion and cosmetic industries to make money.

By this time Larry's eyes were glazing over, but I was glued to her every word. You can only imagine how cool it was to hear an expert talking about the very stuff that keeps me up at night. Not only did she put my innermost thoughts into words, but she made it sound like a well-written SAT essay.

At that moment, everything became clear. Not only was I not a loser because I had zero interest in anything prom-related, but it was my responsibility to warn the students at Castle Heights about how society was trying to brainwash them. It's not like I was hearing *voices* or anything, but I just knew that it was up to me to do something.

Which is why, instead of continuing on to *Sex and the City,* I marched over to my laptop and fired off my letter to Andrea Nuzzo, the *Castle Heights Courier* editor. If there's one area where I'm above-average, it's working with words, which is a good thing, seeing that I plan to be a writer when I grow up. After I pressed send, I turned to the picture of my mom on my desk. "Thanks, Mom," I said.

With her African dashiki shirt and oversize glasses circa

1979, my mother may have looked like fashion roadkill, but I still loved the picture. Almost as much as the one of her and my dad (with matching perms circa 1981) at a Barry Manilow concert during their honeymoon that I kept on my nightstand.

From what my dad told me, my mother had also written her fair share of letters to the editor. She had been a public defender in the Bronx and was pretty opinionated. I know it sounds out there, but I like to think she "helped" me write *my* letters from wherever she now was. I also used to think that she spoke to me through Sushi (my dog, not the food) because I'd ask him questions and he'd answer in a variety of different noises. But that was before he was diagnosed with irritable bowel syndrome. Once he went on medication, the talking stopped. Now he just compulsively licks himself.

As I was e-mailing my letter to Andrea (with blind cc's to India and Malcolm), an IM came through from my friend BklynBoy. As you might guess from his screen name, he lives in Brooklyn. We became e-friends after he wrote me a fan letter last year saying how much he enjoyed my blog *My Life as a Character in an Eighties Teen Comedy*, especially my post entitled "Anatomy of a Sugar Binge." I decided to take the blog down after someone tipped me off to the fact that a girl in Des Moines, Iowa, was plagiarizing me.

BklynBoy: whatcha doin?

AntiPrincess: just finished another letter to the paper.

BklynBoy: wats it about?

AntiPrincess: how the prom causes mucho damage to the psyches of unpopular kids

BklynBoy: ouch. sounds pretty scathing. ur a true braveheart. send me a copy?

AntiPrincess: yup. so did u ask anyone to ur prom yet?

BklynBoy: nah. most of the girls at my school are idiots.

AntiPrincess: what a coincidence. most of the girls at MY school are idiots, too.

BklynBoy: gotta get back to this english paper. talk 2morrow?

AntiPrincess: yeah. nite.

BklynBoy: nite.

You know that movie *When Harry Met Sally*? How they'd do things like call each other late at night and watch movies together? And how when, after ten years of being friends, Billy Crystal realizes he's in love with Meg Ryan and runs fifty blocks on New Year's Eve to tell her and says, "I love that you're the last person I want to talk to before I go to sleep at night?" Well, I feel like that's what might eventually happen with me and BklynBoy—after we both play the field for a few years. Even though we've never actually met, after India and Malcolm, he's my best friend. But I find myself thinking about him more than you would a pseudo best friend you've never met. For instance, I'll hear a song on the radio and think, *Note to self: remember to tell BklynBoy to go to iTunes and check out this band,* or I'll be in 7-Eleven buying gum and think, *Note to self: remember to ask BklynBoy whether he prefers Orbit or Dentyne Ice.* It's sort of like we're boyfriend/girlfriend, but without the boyfriend/girlfriend part.

I'd have a better idea about whether I could ever see myself physically attracted to him if he would agree to send me a picture of himself. After BklynBoy and I had e-mailed a few times, I told him that since he knew what I looked like it was only fair that he send me a picture of him, but he refused, saying that he didn't want my opinion of him to change because of his physical appearance. Malcolm's convinced that's code for "I have a hunchback *and* a lazy eye," but that's just because Malcolm's shallow when it comes to that kind of stuff.

BklynBoy already knew what I looked like from when I still had my blog and had posted some photos of me and Andrew McCarthy from my fifteenth birthday. Not the Andrew McCarthy who lived down the street from me and was semifamous because he had the largest collection of vintage Barbie dolls in the country, but the *really* famous Andrew McCarthy—the one who appeared in many

30

of John Hughes's movies in the eighties. My dad had arranged for me and Malcolm and India to go to the set of Andrew's latest movie—you have no idea what a thrill it was to be thisclose to the guy who played Blane in *Pretty in Pink*. He (BklynBoy, not Andrew McCarthy) said I looked like a "young Kyra Sedgwick" (who is on this show *The Closer*), which I guess isn't a bad thing. Personally I think I look more like a blond Olive Oyl with hair that won't stay straight no matter how many times I use the expensive straightening iron I got for Christmukah last year.

People may not point and scream when they see me, but I'm also not going to win any Miss Castle Heights Class of 2007 pinup contests. Which, unfortunately, is what the boys at Castle Heights want. They're spoiled brats with overinflated senses of entitlement (at least that's what Dr. Greenburg says) and seem to think that if they just hold out long enough, Mandy Moore will soon be throwing herself at them. Not like I ever want to date any of them anyway. Except maybe Adam Silver, but that's never going to happen, seeing that he's the most popular guy in school. I know it's weird that I—Ms. Anti-Prom/Anti-Popularity Girl—would have a crush on someone like that, especially since I've never spoken to him, but I have a feeling that he's really nice. According to India's mother's best friend Sola—a psychic to the stars and occasional *E! True Hollywood Story* correspondent—I'm a very intuitive person. It has something to do with my menstrual cycle.

That night, the minute I closed my eyes, I was out like a light. Usually when I get into bed I have trouble falling asleep and find myself thinking about BklynBoy or Adam Silver, or worrying about whether I spaced on some homework, or if there's any truth to what the Clones say about me being a freak. But when your conscience is clear because not only have you expressed yourself, but you've done it in the name of your fellow humankind, there's no reason to suffer from insomnia.

I like to think I had made my mother proud.

chapter three

The next day, India and Malcolm reminded me that Andrea Nuzzo was going to the prom with Bryan Berkus, so the chances of her sticking out her neck and printing the letter were slim to none. Then, I came up with the idea of starting a competitive newspaper. Mine would be a lot more liberal and hard-hitting—sort of like the *Village Voice* in New York. As Malcolm and I walked to English that afternoon, discussing how his gossip column would push the envelope like no other high school paper had done before, someone tapped me on the shoulder.

"Cindy?"

I turned around to find Andrea Nuzzo, who at 5′ 11″ to my 5′ 3″ towered over me.

"Hey, Andrea, how are you?" I asked.

Not only was she towering—she was glowering. "I got your e-mail. The one with the letter about the . . . *prom*," she hissed.

"Oh, you did?" I said meekly. I wasn't usually such a wimp, but it was hard to tap in to my inner Anderson Cooper when I had a very tall, pissed-off girl whose father may or may not have had ties to the Mafia staring down at me.

"Yeah. I've decided it's going in tomorrow's issue," she said.

"You know, Andrea, I don't want to be disrespectful or anything, because I think that all in all you've done a great job with the paper this year," I began to babble (a lie, I know, but according to Dr. Greenburg, I'm a people pleaser with an overwhelming fear of confrontation), "but I have to tell you I don't understand why you refuse to print *any* of my letters . . . I mean—wait—what?! You're actually going to print it?!" I yelped.

"Yeah."

"But . . . I thought . . . you were going to the prom," I said, dazed.

"I was. At least up until right before lunch," she said, her voice cracking. "When Bryan told me he's decided he'd rather go with Shelby Paxson."

"But I thought Shelby was going with Jason Campbell," Malcolm said.

"She was—up until third period when Jason dumped *her* for Maggie Woolery!" she wailed, tears starting to run down her face. It was like an episode of *Laguna Beach*. "You're right, Gold—the prom is an evil, evil thing. And everyone should know it."

34

Malcolm was almost jumping out of his loafers. "Oh. My. God! This is *so* exciting!"

"Wow. Gosh. I mean . . . wow. Thanks, Andrea," I stuttered.

"Are you going to run a picture with it?" Malcolm asked. "Not that I have any idea how we'd be able to give her a full makeover *and* find a photographer on such short notice, but of course, as her publicist, I'll do my best."

"Publicist?" I asked.

"Of course," he replied. "Someone needs to make sure you don't embarrass yourself now that you're about to become a public figure."

"Why would I run a picture?" Andrea asked.

"Because all columnists have their picture next to their column!" he exclaimed.

Sometimes Malcolm could be so embarrassing I wanted to kill him.

"Hey, she's not getting a *column*. It's just this one letter, got it?" she said.

"Malcolm," I whispered, "stop." If he kept talking he'd talk her right out of printing it. "Thanks again, Andrea," I said. "I really appreciate this op—"

She stomped off before I even finished my sentence. I remembered that line that Ms. McManus, my English teacher, had brought up the other day when we were talking about how the Jen/Brad/Angelina situation was a modern-day Shakespearean tragedy: "Hell hath no fury

35

like a woman scorned." I felt sorry for Andrea, but in this case her heartbreak was my *lucky* break.

Malcolm turned to me. "So how does it feel to know that your life is about to change in a huge way?" he asked.

"Um, good?" I replied as I continued down the hall in a daze. Apparently my gift with words had left the building.

I'm not much of a clotheshorse—my standard outfit consists of jeans, a T-shirt with a witty saying (my current favorite being MY THERAPIST SAYS I'M A GREAT CATCH) and flip-flops—but seeing that I was about to become famous with the publication of the letter, I took extra care with my appearance the next morning. I still wore jeans, a T-shirt, and flip-flops, but I did attempt to straighten my hair, which meant that I kept India waiting for thirty seconds instead of the usual five when she came to pick me up that morning.

"Comeon, comeon, comeon—we don't want to be late!" she yelled out the window as I hustled over to Goldie Hawn, her 1972 VW bus. India is one of those people who freaks out to the *n*th degree when it comes to structure in the school zone—like if she's late to class, or if there's a pop quiz, or (no one can understand this part) if the teacher forgets to give a previously announced quiz. Her therapist, Dr. Lerner, says that her pathological desire for order in the school setting is because she never grew up with any order at home. India's parents are such free spirits that the only thing they've ever insisted on is that she be true to herself and follow her bliss.

"So are you beyond excited?" asked India as she tried to restart Goldie's stalled engine while we held up traffic on Coldwater Canyon on our way to school. A few months earlier, India's dad had decided to enter the new millennium and bought a Toyota Prius, giving her the bus. It broke down a lot, but according to him, it had "really good vibes."

"Yeah, I guess so," I said nervously.

"Hey, maybe you could even get a book deal out of this," she said. "You could call it *From the Sidelines into the Fire: How I Became a Teenage Activist.*" She rolled down her window and stuck her head out. "Sir, I understand you're in a hurry to get to your job, where you'll probably spend the day screaming at your assistant that your coffee isn't the right color," she yelled to the man in the Range Rover in back of us who had his hand permanently attached to his horn, "but I'm trying my best here, so, please, just take this opportunity to breathe and practice patience."

She pulled her head back in the car and got back to the business of trying to start the engine while Mr. Range Rover continued honking and I nervously picked at my cuticles. As we got closer and closer to school, the idea of my life changing so drastically freaked me out more and more. "I doubt all that many people will read the letter. They'll be—" I said.

Before I could finish, India had her head back out the window. "HEY—THAT'S ENOUGH OUTTA YOU, SO JUST CAN IT ALREADY, ALL RIGHT?! YOU'RE NOT THE ONLY ONE WHO'S GOT SOMEWHERE TO BE, MISTER!" she screamed. Once back in, she took a deep breath and smiled sweetly at me. "Sorry. You were saying?"

"I was saying they'll be too busy trying to get every-thing on that prom checklist done," I sputtered. Because it happened so infrequently, watching India freak out like the rest of us tripped me out.

A few minutes later, we pulled in to the parking lot, where India led me through some *ujai* breathing so that I could become centered and ready to take on the world. Castle Heights's campus is much bigger than it needs to be, so the walk from the parking lot to the main building takes a very long time. At first I thought all the stares and whispers were because we were walking behind Jessica Rokosny, the rehab grad, but when it continued even after Jessica went her way and I went mine and then exploded into full-on pointing in homeroom, my stomach sank down to my flip-flops.

"I'm so not going to be able to deal with this fame stuff," I murmured as I took my seat and tried to hide behind my hair, which, thankfully, had returned to its Jew-'fro state.

"I'm impressed, Gold," Larry Goldfarb whispered from behind me.

As much as I didn't like being the center of attention, I couldn't stop the smile that came over my lips. "Thanks," I whispered back as I fiddled with the Tiffany heart necklace that had belonged to my mom.

"Everyone thought you were weird to begin with—but now you're a bona fide *freak* like me," he hissed. As Larry had spent freshman year at one of those wilderness schools for psychopaths-in-the-making, it wasn't exactly a ringing endorsement.

I turned around. "What do you mean 'freak'?"

Before he could answer, Ms. Joyce, our homeroom teacher, click-clacked her way to the front of the room. "Okay, people, settle down," she boomed. Ms. Joyce is what my dad calls a "true broad." A cross between Bette Davis and Katharine Hepburn, she wore old-school pantsuits and high heels every day.

"Okay, before I take attendance, I just want to say that despite the rumors that are going around the teachers' lounge this morning that the bourgeois administration of this school is talking about having the editor of the *Courier* issue an apology regarding a certain letter that appeared in today's issue"—she gave me a pointed look—"I, myself, was thrilled to see them finally print something with *cojones* instead of that crap they usually run."

That was tame for Ms. Joyce. No one knew how she gets away with being so opinionated, although there was talk that she and Mr. Lucchesi, the vice principal, had dated right after his divorce, before he married his twenty-five-year-old Pilates teacher.

Tracee Sampson's hand shot up. "Well, *I* think that the

person who wrote the letter"—another pointed look—"just wrote it because she feels alienated because she refuses to take part in any extracurricular clubs or activities." Tracee is in the Debate, French, Culturally Correct, and Gay/Straight Alliance clubs. I am in the Go Home After School and Watch *My Super Sweet 16* Club.

Ms. Joyce gave her a withering look. "Thank you, Tracee, for weighing in with that bit of startling psychological insight. But enough about that. Time for attendance. Adams?"

"Here . . ."

That was how the entire morning went. At the start of each class, the teacher would make a comment about my letter without mentioning me by name and some kid would add his or her two cents and I would slink down in my seat so that only my head was visible. My personal favorite: in history, when Nick DiFranco, Castle Heights's biggest stoner, said, "Dude, we have a school *newspaper*?! How sweet!"

India was right that I had hit a nerve. People felt strongly about what I had written, but unfortunately, those feelings happened to go *against* what I had written because no one wanted to buck the system. A few of the teachers were supportive, like Ms. Joyce, but for the most part, everyone thought that the letter was just the work of some bitter, maladjusted kid rather than a nice Jewish girl.

It wasn't like I was about to get on top of the building with a machine gun. I was just trying to express myself. But L.A.'s a city that's all about image. It's a town whose main business is make-believe (i.e., movies and television—including reality TV), so it made sense that everyone wanted to believe in happy endings, complete with a ball and a prince and a glass slipper.

After wiping the graffiti off my locker after lunch, I headed to study hall. "Of course you're right," whispered Simone Shapiro when I asked her for her take on the whole thing. Simone is a junior and, with her pierced bottom lip and four tattoos, definitely one of the more "expressive" kids at Castle Heights. "But it's not like you can change things. Everyone here has been programmed at birth to want to fit in and be popular."

"That's exactly my point," I whispered back. "Like I said in my letter, the beauty and fashion industries are evil." As evidenced by the fact that almost every girl in study hall had her head buried in a glossy fashion magazine, apparently that memo hadn't made it to Castle Heights.

Simone laughed. "I'm talking about being programmed by their *parents*. Take my mom, for instance. My dad calls her the homecoming queen of Montana Avenue." Montana is a street in ritzy Santa Monica that's known for overpriced boutiques. "She's been talking about the prom since I was six."

"Hey, why don't *you* write a letter in response to my

letter?" I suggested. "I know you said it's pointless to try and change things, but it only takes two people to try to build a village." I love mixing and matching famous sound bites. "Oh my God, I have an even better idea: we can stage a sit-in outside the prom!" I said excitedly. "You know, like a human chain. I'll ask Wally to come with his guitar and play 'We Shall Overcome'!" Visions of being on the front page of the *Los Angeles Times* filled my head: I'd be the first antiprom activist the city had ever seen.

"Are you nuts?" asked Simone. "My dad would kill me if I did something like that. They'd probably kick him out of Hillhurst." Hillhurst is one of the big country clubs in town. "Plus Doug would kill me—he's campaigning for us to win Prom King and Queen."

I sighed and went back to my geometry homework, feeling as square as the rhombus in front of me. You knew you were in trouble when not even Simone Shapiro—who had self-published a book of poetry about the alienation that the transgendered feel, even though she didn't even *know* anyone who was transgendered— would back you up.

By the time I got home that afternoon, the shock of becoming the new school leper had settled in to a not-so-unpleasant numbness.

Spencer and I were in the family room mechanically shoving chocolate chip cookies in our mouths and watching

Dr. Phil humiliate an overweight twelve-year-old girl. In order to drown out our housekeeper Evelin's vacuuming, I had the volume turned up to eardrum-shattering, which made the whole experience even more traumatic.

As the girl broke down into tears, I saw the Clones' Saab coming up the driveway.

"Okay, Spence, you gotta back me up here if the Clones start in on me," I said as I placed him on the floor with what I vowed would be his last cookie no matter how much he whined. *Maybe they won't think the letter was such a big deal,* I thought as I sank even farther down into the overstuffed sofa pillows. I loved that couch. It was the most comfortable couch on the planet: buttery brown suede with overstuffed down pillows. And, finally, a year after getting it, Clarissa was allowing us to sit on it, even though she constantly reminded us that it was "almost too expensive" to do so.

The aggressive click-clacking (Ashley) and flip-flopping (Britney) coming down the hall made it clear that perhaps the Clones *did* think the letter was a bigger deal than I would have hoped.

Within seconds, I could feel two pairs of ice blue eyes glaring at me from the doorway while I kept my own green ones focused on the plasma television screen.

"Cindy?" I heard Ashley say.

I turned around and blinked a few times like you see people do in movies when they're trying to look surprised. "Hey, Ash; hey, Brit—I didn't hear you come in."

They didn't look numb; they looked pissed.

"So what's up? I didn't see you guys around campus today," I lied. I had seen them trying to pretend *they* didn't see *me* as I walked from French to geometry that morning. It was great to be able to count on family in times of crisis.

"So are you gonna tell us what that whole thing was about?" demanded Britney.

"What what whole thing was about?" I asked as I moved the bag of cookies away from Spencer, who had managed to get his overalls off and was now wearing only his T-shirt and diaper. Not only aren't we allowed to eat anywhere outside of the kitchen, but Clarissa had recently announced a no-refined sugar rule in the household, so if she came home early from Yoga Booty Ballet and caught me, I'd be doubly screwed.

"The. Letter. To. The. Editor," snipped Ashley. A few months ago Ashley. Had. Taken. To. Talking. Like. That. when she was pissed off, which meant that getting reamed out by her took twice the time it needed to.

"Ohh, you mean the thing in the *Courier!*" I said.

They nodded in unison, like stars of *The Stepford Barbie Girls*.

"It was just, you know, a few thoughts I came up with the other night. Did you like it?" I asked hopefully.

They looked at me like I was crazy.

"You. *Totally*. Humiliated. Us," said Ashley. "Big. Time."

They felt humiliated? I wanted to tell them to try living in my skin for the last eight hours, but I doubted that would go over well.

"Remember how we talked about how even though you're not related to us and our mom will probably end up divorcing your dad at some point because she's got major commitment issues, you're still a reflection on us?" asked Britney as she jealously eyed the bag of cookies.

"Yeah."

"Well, this is, like, *totally* not the reflection we want you to be giving," said Ashley. "I knew that invention we did last week wasn't strong enough." She pouted.

"You know, I really don't understand why everyone's making such a big deal about this," I said as I finished the last of the cookies. "It's just a stupid letter in a stupid school newspaper. It's not like it ended up in *Teen Vogue* or anything like that."

"That's not the point," said Britney. "The point is that it's full of lies!"

"What kind of lies?" I asked.

"Like the fact that the prom is some kind of huge popularity contest or something!" said Ashley. "It's totally not. It's just an event where kids get to dress up and celebrate—"

"Being popular?" I said.

She looked confused. "Well, yeah. Kind of."

"Ashley . . . " warned Britney. "I'll handle this." Britney

was the winner of most of the brain cells in the womb. "What you did was *totally* uncool, Cin."

"Yeah," agreed Ashley. "You were uncool to begin with, but with this you went above and below."

"She means 'beyond,' " clarified Britney. "We're going to have to do some serious damage control with this one, Cindy. You better hope something really juicy happens soon so that people move on to something else," she warned.

"It's not like I wrote it to embarrass you guys," I said defensively.

"Then why *did* you do it?" asked Ashley.

"I did it to express myself."

"How many times do we need to tell you: you'd be a lot better off if you stopped doing that," said Britney.

"Yeah," agreed Ashley. "Like maybe then you'd actually have a social life."

"C'mon, Ash," huffed Britney. "I can't even be in the same room with her right now."

As they click-clacked and flip-flopped their way out, the numbness from earlier turned to confusion. I guess I *was* setting myself up for a fall with the letter, but I didn't think it was going to be from fifty stories. Maybe Dr. Greenburg was wrong about self-expression being a healthy thing. And maybe everyone else was right: maybe the reason I wrote the letter *was* that I was bitter because I wasn't popular and I didn't have a boyfriend and other than this kid Jeff Katz from camp last year, I had never even kissed a guy. Thankfully no one but India and Malcolm knew that last part.

As I watched the overweight girl and her anorexic mother share a tearful embrace, I marveled at how neatly things wrapped up on TV. While Dr. Phil gloated beside them, the two of them looked so sure of themselves, certain that life would now be a piece of cake (well, in the overweight girl's case, a piece of fruit). But me? That afternoon all I wanted was for the ozone layer to finish disappearing overnight so I wouldn't have to go to school the next day.

"Spencer, listen up, because I'm about to give you the most important advice you'll ever receive," I said as I tried to refasten his diaper, which was now three-quarters of the way off. "If you can swing it, I would suggest you avoid growing up at all costs."

Because some days sure were a lot harder than others.

chapter four

The good news about having a domestically challenged stepmother and a workaholic father is that family dinners are kept to a minimum, so I was able to hide out in my room that night and avoid more "you've ruined our lives" accusations from the Clones. Clarissa and my dad were at a screening of the latest film based on a hit TV show from the seventies, so I didn't have to deal with her, either, which was a relief. Once the Clones filled her in on the letter, my butt would be gluten-free toast.

With the help of some who-knows-how-old chocolate I found in my nightstand and an IM pep talk with BklynBoy (*"Look at it this way: homeschooling's in at the moment"*) I made it through the night. Well, I made it until 3:30 A.M. when I was woken up by killer cramps and the discovery that I had just gotten my period (all over my white cotton pajamas thankyouverymuch) and couldn't get back to sleep.

The next day, armed with enough maxi pads to make my own king-size feather bed, I returned to Castle Heights High for yet another chapter of *Starring Cindy E. Gold as Joan of Arc.* That morning during announcements, Mrs. Anton, the principal, informed the school that despite a certain letter that had appeared in the *Courier,* all but two seniors would be showing their Castle Heights spirit and had bought their tickets for the prom, which meant that the senior Untouchables must have broken down and asked one another. Everyone figured that one of the nonpromgoers had to be Eddie Chin because he was in a coma after contracting bird flu during a visit to his grandmother in China, but no one knew who the other person was. Not to sound like an egomaniac, but I hoped that whoever that other person was, his or her decision not to attend was in the teensiest part because of my letter.

The good news was that my cramps were so bad that I couldn't focus on anything else, like all those dirty looks.

"Maybe you *should* try and get yourself a column somewhere. Now that you're somewhat famous," suggested India as we waited in line to adopt a refugee at lunch. The Culturally Correct Club was doing a fund-raiser where, for ten dollars a month, you'd receive a letter from a kid from some war-torn country thanking you for feeding him and his entire village for the next month while you felt guilty about the fact that you lived in a house with running water and Wi-Fi.

I snorted. "Oh yeah? What am I gonna call it? *Notes from a Teenage Pariah?*"

"Hey, there's a lot of people who think what you did was great," said India.

"Like who?"

"Like . . . those Nerds For Jesus who came up to you in the parking lot this morning. I think it's awesome that they asked you to be the key speaker during their annual baptism week."

I knew India was just trying to help, but I couldn't stand the way yoga people always insisted on looking at the bright side of things.

"Let's talk about something else. This is way too depressing." I sighed as I picked up the catalog of available adoptees and started flipping through it. "So do I want a seven-year-old Sri Lankan girl or an eight-year-old Sudanese boy?" I asked.

"I don't know. I'm having trouble deciding whether I want mine to have a missing limb or just be severely malnourished," she replied.

I put my catalog down. "Okay, this is even *more* depressing. I'm going to the bathroom. I'll meet you outside."

They say bad things happen in threes, and it was as I was on my way to the bathroom that the third bad thing showed up (the first two being the letter and my period). Because as I made my way down the deserted hallway, who was walking toward me but Adam Silver, my semisecret crush.

I had often fantasized about something like this happening: the two of us finding ourselves alone in a room, away from the crowds of gorgeous girls that seemed to follow him everywhere, so he could see me up close and realize that he was face-to-face with his soul mate. But it wasn't supposed to happen after I had just been crowned "Loser of the Year" and had period pimples.

"Just great," I mumbled as I trudged down the hall, making sure to keep my eyes on my feet rather than risk turning red if I looked up and saw the way his sun-kissed brown hair flopped oh-so-perfectly in his milk-chocolate-brown eyes.

The thing about staring at your shoes while you're walking is that you're unable to see where you're going, which means if, say, there's a bank of water fountains in your path, you end up bumping into them. And if your book bag isn't zippered like, say, mine never is, it'll probably go sailing across the hall and everything will fall out of it. Including any maxi pads you may have stashed in there.

Bad things didn't happen in threes. They happened in fours.

"Are you, uh, okay?" a voice asked as I tried to pick myself up off the floor. Along with the book bag, I, too, had gone sailing across the hall.

I prayed that somehow, in the few moments between

the water fountain and my fall, Adam Silver had left the hallway and that the husky voice belonged not to Adam, but to someone who had just transferred to Castle Heights that morning and therefore hadn't yet been briefed on my avoid-at-all-cost status. But when I looked up into those brown eyes that I now saw weren't just brown, but also had cool flecks of gold in them, I realized that I had the starring role in the latest Hollywood blockbuster horror movie.

"Yeah, I'm fine," I mumbled, scrambling to pick up the maxi pads, sitting there, right next to his scuffed Pumas.

"Are you sure? That was a pretty gnarly wipeout."

Oh my God. That voice . . . it was better in person than it had ever sounded in my daydreams.

"Happens all the time," I said as I scooped up the Kotex along with my toothbrush and toothpaste and dental floss (I never leave home without it). "See, I'm fine," I said as I stood up and winced, wondering whether I had broken my tailbone. I looked up at him. Now was my chance to say something—*anything*—to make an impression on him, because God knows I'd never have the chance again. I took a deep breath and summoned up all my courage.

"Bye," I said as I limped off.

The rest of the day was a piece of cake. There was no way I could be any more humiliated than having just embarrassed myself in front of the guy that I secretly hoped to marry because then we'd be "Gold and Silver," which was beyond cute. (There's no way I am changing my name when I get married. Naomi and all those other feminists worked way too hard for me to give up my identity. Plus, I'll probably already be a famous novelist by then, so I don't want to confuse people.)

That evening, my cramps were still so bad that I had to bow out of going to the New Beverly with Malcolm and India for the *Sixteen Candles/Pretty in Pink* double feature.

"Really? They're that bad?" Malcolm asked when I called him to cancel.

"Yeah. And the bruise on my butt isn't helping," I said, stretched out on my bed with an ice pack under my butt and a heating pad on my stomach.

"This isn't a cry for help, is it?" he asked worriedly. "You're not planning on *hurting* yourself, are you?"

"Oh God. Have you been talking to Clarissa? Why would I hurt myself?"

"Um, maybe because everyone except me, India, and the Nerds For Jesus have written you off as an Untouchable and you'll spend the rest of your high school career recovering from this?" he asked. "Let's face it, that would put a damper on anyone's day."

"Thanks for breaking it down so clearly. But to answer your question, no, I won't be hurting myself over this. I may eat a little more chocolate than usual, but that's partly because of my period."

"Cindy Ella?" Clarissa yelled from downstairs.

"Gotta go," I said. "Call me with any D-list star sightings." Last time we went to the New Beverly we had four D-list star sightings, probably because they show only old movies and have uncomfortable seats. I found D-list sightings much more interesting than A-list sightings, anyway. Anyone could go to Teddy's or Area and see Jessica Biel or Paris Hilton, but to see Shannen Doherty or Tiffani Amber-Thiessen from *Beverly Hills 90210*? Now, *that* was exciting.

When I got downstairs, a diaper-clad Spencer kept trying to grab at Clarissa's skirt as she continued to sidestep him and apply yet another coat of lipstick to her already shellacked lips in front of the full-length mirror in the foyer.

"Now, Cindy Ella," she said as she tried not to get lipstick on her upper lip. "Obviously now's not the time to have this conversation because I have to go meet your daddy at some Save the Extinct Animals of L.A. benefit, but the girls showed me that article you wrote for the paper and I'm"—she turned away from the mirror and flashed me what passed for a disturbed look in Clarissaland— "*very disturbed* about this." She turned back to the mirror. "In fact, I think I'm going to call Dr. Gerstein and ask him if I should call Dr. Greenburg and talk to him about this before your next session."

"It wasn't an article. It was a letter to the editor," I clarified.

"Well, whatever it was, it was *very disturbing.*" She turned toward Spencer and pointed her lipstick tube at him. "Spencer, honey, *no*—don't do that. Keep your diaper *on.*"

Spencer ignored her and started crawling butt naked toward the family room, where the Wiggles could be heard jamming away.

She turned back to me. "Where was I? Oh, right— Cindy Ella, those were some *very strong* words you used. Not to mention the fact that it was some *very passive-aggressive* acting out toward your stepsisters. I'm *very worried* about this, Cindy Ella. You know, last year there was a Lifetime movie where a girl just like you, with good grades, and a beautiful house, and a loving family— she even had a pony—ended up taking an overdose of her mother's Valium because she was so unhappy at school."

"I'm not unhappy at school," I corrected her.

"Yes, you are. Or else you wouldn't have written such a disturbing article."

"Letter to the editor," I corrected her again.

"Cindy Ella, whether it's an article, or a letter or a screenplay, is not the issue here. The issue is that you're severely unhappy *and,* with this letter, you've embarrassed your stepsisters, who've done nothing but try and bond with you over the years. You've been in therapy much too long for you to act out like this. Now, I have to leave or else I'll miss the silent auction—which is the only good part about these things—but I'd like you to give this whole thing some serious thought after you've fed Spencer and given him a bath, and put him to bed and we'll discuss it first thing in the morning." She started fluffing my hair. "Okay, sugar?"

"Okay," I said. Maybe she'd be so excited about whatever she won at the silent auction that she'd forget about the letter.

"Oh, and Sushi needs to be fed as well."

"Okay."

"And Evelin forget to load the dishwasher and fold the laundry that's in the dryer, so if you could do that, it would be a big help to her."

"Okay," I said again. I had shown Clarissa how to use the dishwasher and washer and dryer over and over, but she always seemed to forget how to turn them on.

"Wonderful. Kiss kiss," she said as she strolled out the door in a wake of heavy perfume.

After Spencer, Sushi, and I split a Stouffer's French Bread Pizza, I gave Spencer his bath, put him to bed, and then went to clean my room. A wild and crazy Friday night, but I can't stand clutter. Dr. Greenburg said that my need for order was understandable in light of the childhood trauma I'd undergone. It's not like I'm obsessive-compulsive about neatness—just very organized. For instance, all my DVDs and books are not only alphabetized, but are also lined up by the year they were released. And all the postcards of famous women whom I admire—like Joni Mitchell, Jennifer Aniston, and J. K. Rowling—are equally spaced out on my bulletin board. Gwyneth Paltrow used to be up there, but then I read an interview where she came off as really stuck-up, so I took her down.

With my "Friday Night & Alone Again Naturally" playlist (My Chemical Romance, Dashboard Confessional, Fall Out Boy, etc.) keeping me company, I went online to update my MySpace page and delete the day's "Ur a FREAK Cindy Ella Gold" posts before going to Adam Silver's for clues to his innermost thoughts (and to check that he didn't write anything about the loser girl who had wiped out in front of him that afternoon), but other than a play-by-play recap of the Dodger game the night before, there was nothing new.

BklynBoy wasn't around because it was Friday night and he *had* a life, so I got into bed with the one photo album I had from when I was a kid. Looking at pictures of my life B.M.D. (Before Mom Died) always made me feel better, reminding me that there had once been a time when I had felt . . . normal. Before I lost my mom and everything changed. My dad tried his best, but having to stand there as he asked the clerk at Rite Aid to explain the difference between Kotex maxi pads and Stayfree panty liners was almost as painful as losing my mom. Obviously I'm joking—which is how

I defend myself against the pain of the abandonment complex that manifested itself after her death, which was then exacerbated by my father marrying a woman who withholds her love from me. Well, at least that's what Dr. Greenburg says. To be honest, I have no idea what he's talking about half the time.

As I flipped through pictures of my parents looking fascinated by me lying in my crib like a bump on a log, or me and my mom picking apples at an orchard, or feeding the ducks at a park, I wondered what my life would have been like if she was still around. Would we even live in L.A.? Somehow I doubt it. And if we did, I bet she would've insisted on sending me to a public magnet school where prom dresses didn't cost as much as a down payment on a condo. And she'd probably frame the letter instead of worrying that it was a cry for help.

Even though Dr. Greenburg and I had talked a lot about how difficult it was to be your own person when everyone around you was trying to be just like the person next to them, *knowing* it was hard didn't make it any easier. I shut the photo album and looked up at the ceiling. "Are You there, God? It's me, Cindy," I said out loud.

Nada.

I looked over at Sushi, who, thanks to the Stouffer's French Bread Pizza, was passed out cold. I had found that back when he was still making all those noises, Sushi had been able to channel God as well as my mom.

"Okay, well, maybe You're not. Who knows. But if You are, I just wanted to say that if there's any way You could give me a sign that I haven't screwed up my life with that letter, I'd really appreciate it. It doesn't have to be a *huge* sign, but if You could make it enough of one so that I'm sure not to miss it, or, you know, confuse it as a sign of something else, that would be great."

Still nothing.

"Okay. Well, thanks anyway. Bye," I said uncomfortably. Talking to God freaks me out, but in case it works like all those people on the Sunday-morning Bible shows swear it does, I don't want to miss out.

The combination of being ignored by God and getting to the pictures of my bald-but-smiling postchemo mom was too depressing to continue, so I shut the album and decided to call it a night.

After, of course, a thorough round of brushing, flossing, and face washing. An early childhood full of filmstrips about the dangers of unbrushed teeth, followed by stern lectures by Mrs. Hall, our middle school health teacher, on how improper hygiene would quickly turn our shiny little faces into acne minefields, had put the fear of God in me.

I was in the bathroom happily flossing away when I heard my IM beep and ran back into the bedroom, eager to hear who Malcolm and India had spied at the movies.

BklynBoy: can't really talk b/c out w/friends but wanted to check in and see how ur doing . . . and say i think ur letter was awesome. later.

Okay, so it wasn't a huge sign. It was more like a medium sign, and it came from three thousand miles away, but it was enough of one for me.

chapter five

The next morning I came downstairs to find Clarissa and the Clones staked out at the kitchen table in front of the phone, pushing the redial button, while Spencer, in his high chair, copied them on his Fisher-Price one.

"Morning," I said as I made my way through our kitchen, which resembled a Martha Stewart set. Why Clarissa had insisted on a $5,000 Viking stove and copper pans hanging from the ceiling when all she did was defrost or warm up tofu dishes was beyond me.

No answer. Clarissa was so focused on what she was doing that a very un-Botox-like crease had shown up between her eyebrows.

"What's going on?" I asked as I joined them at the table with my carrot juice (one of Ashley's faves when on her Orange Foods diet) and a no-sugar-no-wheat-no-taste cranberry muffin.

"We found out last night at Laura Miller's sushi barbecue

that not only is Dylan going to be wearing a Jaden, but now Maisie Broderick and Madison Smallwood are, too," explained Britney as she eyed my muffin jealously before glancing down at her flat stomach as if to convince herself there was a method to the madness of denying herself.

"Which is, like, *totally* unacceptable, as far as we're concerned," added Ashley. "So Mom's going to get Jaden on the phone and blackmail her into making us ones, too."

"Ashley, honey, I told you, it's *not* blackmail," said Clarissa.

"It's checking in with a long-lost friend and reminding her of old times, right?" I asked.

"Exactly," agreed Clarissa as she kept punching away at the redial button.

"Where's my dad?" I asked as I started picking at the muffin.

"At work, silly. It's Saturday," Clarissa replied. He didn't go in *every* Saturday, but he did go in on a lot of them, at least for the morning.

"So I guess you're going to drive me over to Larchmont, then?" I asked.

"What's at Larchmont?"

"The new tutor. At ten. Remember? And since it's my first time meeting him, I should probably be early rather than late." I hate to be late. Dr. Greenburg says there is some psychological meaning behind it, but I can't remember what it is.

Even though I wasn't taking the SATs for another year, my dad had insisted that I start studying for them early so I could get into an Ivy League school. So then I could be under huge pressure and develop an eating disorder? No thanks. My grades were decent enough—A's and B's—but I already knew where I was going: NYU. And if I didn't get in there, I'd go to one of those crunchy granola schools where they don't believe in grades. Plus, when I sold the movie rights to my first novel for a million dollars, none of it would matter anyway.

"Right. I forgot. But if it doesn't work out with this one, you're done," she warned.

My first tutor had been a guy named Ahmet. He was pretty cool, but Clarissa had a cow when she found out that we were spending more time deciding what songs his band, Scarlett Johansson's Lips, should play at an upcoming Battle of the Bands rather than reviewing algebra word problems. Hopefully, Noah, the new one, would be just as cool.

"Fine with me," I said as I finished my muffin and got up to get a bowl of Cinnamon Life cereal. A growing girl couldn't possibly get by with a measly five-calorie muffin, especially when forced to use her brain cells on a Saturday studying Latin verb roots and isosceles triangles. Ashley watched my carb fest with fascination. "Want some?" I asked, holding up my spoon.

She scooted her chair back and shook her head.

Finally Clarissa's button punching paid off and the bleating busy signal was replaced with a ringing sound.

"Jaden! Sugar! It's Clarissa Gold," she drawled as she took the phone off speaker. "How *are* you, darlin'?" Her semismile faded. "Clarissa *Gold*," she said. "From that Tuesday morning AA women's meeting we used to go to at the church on Santa Monica and Roxbury?"

Pause.

"Oh, sugar, how silly of me—of course you don't know who the hell I am!" she trilled. "Back then I was Clarissa *Dickenson*!"

Another pause.

"Hmm . . . . was it that long ago that I was still Clarissa *Turner*?" she said.

Jaden responded and Clarissa's semismile returned. "Yes, exactly—the one who was with you the first time you made it through Neiman's without shoplifting! So how are you? You can't swing a dead cat without hitting a magazine that has an article about you nowadays."

I sighed as I took Spencer out of his high chair and set him on the floor so he could play with Sushi. So much for being on time for my tutoring session. Clarissa could be very charming when she wanted to be, so there was no telling how long the buttering-up portion of the phone call would go on.

As the two women compared notes on how they had both come to the conclusion that, really, they weren't alcoholics and drug addicts, and that AA had just been a phase, I kept glancing worriedly at the time.

"Um, Clarissa?" I whispered, "We're going to be late." I could feel my stomach starting to clench.

She put her finger to her lips to shush me.

After promising that she wouldn't dream of calling *Star* magazine, Clarissa asked if Jaden might be able to find some time in her busy schedule to whip up some dresses for her two daughters to wear to their prom.

"Tell her I want mine to be really low-cut, like the one Jessica Alba wore to the Nickelodeon Kids' Choice Awards last month," said Ashley.

"I will, sweetie," promised Clarissa.

"And I want mine to be strapless, like the one Kelly Clarkson wore to the Grammys last year," said Britney.

"Yes, baby," she soothed.

"Clarissa?" I said a little louder. "Remember you said you were going to drive me to the tutor?"

Another shush, this time with feeling.

The Clones continued to pepper Clarissa with their demands about what the dresses should and should not look like while I kept glancing at the clock.

"Clarissa?" I tried again. "The tutor? Remember?"

"Jaden, I'm sorry—can you hold on a moment, please?" Clarissa asked. The Southern sweetness was replaced with an icy tone. "Cindy Ella. Can you *not* see I'm in the middle of something?"

"Yeah, but—"

"And is it not obvious that what I'm in the middle of is *extremely* important?" she demanded.

How to answer without getting her more pissed off. "Um . . . I guess, but—"

"I've had just about enough of this acting out, Cindy Ella. Just because you won't be going to the prom doesn't mean you need to ruin it for the rest of us. Am I being clear?"

How could I even attempt to argue with someone like that? So I didn't. I just picked up my SAT book and walked (okay, there was a little stomping mixed in) out to the garage.

With the Clones' Saab convertible, Clarissa's Escalade, and my dad's motorcycle (a token of his short-but-corny midlife crisis) crammed in there, there was barely any room for my bike. Not that I used it all that often (biking equals physical exercise). But since L.A.'s transit system leaves a lot to be desired, it was my only way to get to Larchmont Boulevard, which is where the Starbucks was where I was meeting Noah the Tutor. Thankfully it was only five blocks away, so chances were I wouldn't have a heart attack.

If I *had* enjoyed bike riding, I couldn't have asked for a nicer route. While Brentwood and Santa Monica are full of Spanish-style houses and big-name celebrities, the tree-lined streets of Hancock Park are a lot more charming and low-key. It's so pretty that some days you forget you live in a sprawling, multicultural metropolis. At least until a rap-blaring Hummer drives by.

By the time I got to Larchmont ten minutes later, I was covered with sweat and my curls had turned into a Jew 'fro. Because it was Saturday, the street was overrun with families eating breakfast at one of the many cute cafés, so I had to park my bike one block over on Lucerne and then run back, getting even sweatier as I dodged double strollers. By the time I got to Starbucks, I felt like Pigpen from *Charlie Brown* and I'm sure I smelled like him. It was a good thing I was so antiprom, because looking the way I did that morning, I wouldn't have even been able to get a date with a student from a School for the Blind.

Once inside, I skimmed the crowd of wannabe screenwriters typing furiously on their laptops, looking for Noah. Every Starbucks in town had its own vibe and the Larchmont one—being less "scene-y" and more intellectual than, say, the one on Sunset and Fairfax near India's house, where all the CW-looking actors and actresses hung out—was full of writers. Obviously, as an aspiring best-selling novelist, I preferred this one. If forced to go to Starbucks, that is. Usually I tried to avoid all chains so I couldn't be accused of contributing to corporate America.

I picked Noah out of the crowd right away. Not only because he and a toothless bag lady were the only two in the place without laptops, but because he happened to have the same SAT study guide as I did in front of him—

the one with the cover of a bunch of smiling culturally diverse kids.

Just then, it happened. For the second time in two weeks, I had a major life-altering moment. The minute I set eyes on Noah, I could tell without a shadow of a doubt that he was my soul mate/future husband/father of my children.

It was *that* magical.

More so than anyone I had ever met in real life or seen on TV, Noah was absolutelypositivelyonehundredandfifty percent my type: seminerd cute. You know, the kind of guy who gets cuter as you get to know him, never the other way around? Seminerds aren't popular like Adam Silver, but they definitely know the Adam Silvers of the world because they let the Adams copy their trig homework. They're cool in that intellectual, New York-y way, which is probably why I'm so drawn to them. If Noah was a movie star, he would have been . . . Zach Braff. Or Adam Brody back in his *O.C.* days.

Thankfully he was busy reading *Spin* (seminerds always have cutting-edge taste in music) and therefore didn't see my mouth fall open. The way he kept pushing his dark brown hair out of his eyes (seminerds are always in desperate need of a haircut) was giving me butterflies.

I took a few deep breaths. *Are You there, God? It's me, Cindy,* I said to myself as I stepped over and around various laptop cords and made my way to the table. *If it's not too much trouble, do You think You might be able to give me some flirting skills by the time I get over there?* If flirting were a subject in school, I would've gotten a D-minus. I just didn't get the rationale behind those "Ten Ways to Make Him Melt" articles in *CosmoGIRL!*. Why should you pretend you can't open a door for yourself or wait two days to call a guy back? Total waste of time in my book. But that was B.N. (Before Noah). Suddenly I would've paid big money to be able to Make Him Melt and Make Him Mine when I sat down.

Just before I got to the table, a new song on the Starbucks sound system began. As far as I was concerned, the fact that it was Ella Fitzgerald's "Let's Do It (Let's Fall in Love)" wasn't only a sign, but the best sign I could have ever asked for. My namesake singing about falling in love? It was like God was screaming "YES, CINDY, HE *IS* YOUR SOUL MATE!" in my ear.

"Um, are you, uh, Noah?" I mumbled, staring at his faded Velvet Underground T-shirt. While God may have given me a sign, He/She/It had forgotten the flirting skills.

The man who I was sure would one day be the father of my children looked up at me with the bluest eyes I had ever seen. "Yeah. Are you Cindy?"

I flashed a big white fresh-breathed smile—I knew my compulsive dental hygiene would come in handy at some point—and kept nodding like a non-English-speaking tourist.

"I guess that means yes," he said, smiling back with straight white teeth. "We were scheduled to meet at ten, right?"

"Huh?" I said dreamily, already busy defending our age difference in my head to my dad. Noah looked to be about twenty-two. But a *young*-looking twenty-two. And six and a half years wasn't a crime, especially if I waited until a reasonable age to lose my virginity. When I was twenty-two, he'd only be twenty-seven and a half. And when I was thirty and a half, he'd be thirty-seven. And when I was thirty-five, he'd be—

" . . . it doesn't give us much time—" he said.

"Sure it does," I assured him. *Look at Catherine Zeta-Jones and Michael Douglas,* I wanted to say. *They're like* thirty *years apart.*

"We have an hour and a half," he replied.

"What?" I asked, confused.

"The tutoring sessions are two hours," he said slowly. Maybe he *did* think English was my second language.

Oh. Right. He was there to tutor me.

"Why don't you sit down?" he said, pointing to the chair across from him.

"Ah, that's okay, I'll just stand," I said. I didn't want to take any chances that Noah would see my underwear pop out of my jeans, especially since I had on my yucky period pair.

"You really want to stand for the next hour and a

half?" he asked. He had a great voice—smooth, but a bit nasally. Seminerds were notorious for suffering from allergies and asthma.

"Okay, I'll sit," I said, flashing him a smile. So much for coming across as independent and sure of myself.

"Do you want something to drink before we start?" he asked.

"Oh. Um, yeah." I started rummaging in my backpack for my wallet.

"I've got it—don't worry about it," he said. "What would you like?" Not only was he a gentleman, but he had money. Clarissa would be impressed.

"A mocha Frappuccino?" I said.

"You got it. I'll be right back."

I tried not to stare at how cute his butt looked in his Levi's (perfectly faded, natch) and instead took the opportunity to attempt to de-fro my hair and examine my CELEBRITY IN MY OWN MIND T-shirt for any stains. I was quickly discovering there was a lot to do when you liked a guy.

My heart was leaping around in my chest like a fish that had had one too many Red Bulls. I had never felt this way about a boy since . . . the day before when I was staring into Adam Silver's eyes after the maxi-pad incident. However, seeing that Adam and I were dating only in the music video that played in my mind and not in real life, it wasn't like I was being unfaithful or anything by falling for Noah.

"Sorry for being late," I said when he returned with

my drink. "There was a whole prom-dress to-do going on at my house." I tried my hardest to sip daintily instead of slurp. "Nothing to do with *me* . . . it was about the Clones . . . I mean, my stepsisters . . . I'm not even going to the prom . . . I'm only a sophomore," I stammered. "Not that I couldn't go if I was asked . . . " I realized I was having a Disclosure of Inappropriate Information flare-up, and once they started they were almost impossible to stop. "But because of this letter to the editor I wrote for our school paper about how stupid the prom is and how it puts all this pressure on kids, I don't think that's going to be happening anytime soon." *Please. Shut up right now,* I thought to myself. My face was as red as the Tazo Passion tea that Noah had on the table in front of him.

A smile flickered over his face before he raised his hand to his chin (which had the cutest little cleft) and tried to look serious. "The prom as an agent of stress in today's society," he said. "Interesting."

"Yeah, I thought so, too. But no one else at my dumb school did," I replied as I shifted my chair in order to block Noah's view of the hot-bodied, glowing yoginis who had recently arrived. "Now I'm even more unpopular than Mitchell Frederick—and he's the most unpopular kid in school."

He laughed. "You know, most visionaries *aren't* popular. At least not until years later. Take Kafka, for instance," Noah said.

"Who?"

"Franz Kafka. He wrote *The Metamorphosis*?"

"Oh yeah . . . the story about the giant ant," I said. "We read that last year in AP English."

"Actually, it was a cockroach."

"Right. Of course. I always get my insects mixed up," I said, my cheeks flushing an even deeper red. *Note to self,* I thought. *Make sure to read the Cliffs Notes for all classics before our next tutoring session.*

"Or Emily Dickinson," he said. "Did you know that only seven of her poems were published during her lifetime?"

"Uh, no. Wow," I said. "Hey, you're not a writer by any chance, are you?"

"Yeah. Mainly short stories so far. But I'm also working on a novel."

If that didn't show we were meant to be together, I don't know what did. We could go on book tours together! I was so glad he didn't say he was a screenwriter because *everyone* in L.A. is a screenwriter. My dad always said that 99.9 percent of the screenplays floating around town were horrible, but once in a while you came across one that was good. Like Malcolm's, for example. He had written a sequel to *Sixteen Candles* called *Sixteen More Candles* and it was fantastic. Hysterical, but with heart. Plus, India and I thought his idea to have Molly Ringwald jump-start her career by starring in it was beyond brilliant.

"I'm a writer, too. Well, I mean, I'm *going* to be a writer," I said shyly.

He smiled. "Maybe you'll let me read something sometime."

"Oh no. I mean, none of it is any good. Just some really stupid poetry and, of course, the letters to the editor. This was the first one they printed, but I've written a bunch."

"So you're an activist. That's great."

"Well, not really. It's just a way for me to express myself. My shrink says it's very important that I do that because I have a very rich inner life and that if I don't find a way to creatively express it, I'll explode. Or maybe it's *im*plode. I can never remember," I said. "So anyway, the reason I'm late is because I ended up having to ride my bike because Clarissa—she's my stepmother—was blackmailing this famous designer into making dresses for the Clones. I mean, my stepsisters. That's why I'm all sweaty. But I promise I'll never be late again," I said. "Or sweaty."

"Well, you know, prom-dress emergencies are pretty high up on the potential disaster scale," he said. "I guess I'll have to let it slide this time."

"Thanks." I smiled as I tried to cock my head and slouch sexily the way Mischa Barton always did, but all that happened was that the tip of my ponytail fell into my Frappuccino. "Whoops," I said as I wrung my hair out. So much for trying to look cute.

Noah proved to be even more cool when he

suggested we spend the next hour getting to know each other rather than trying to figure out what time Jimmy would get into Duluth from Iowa City if he was on a train going eighty miles per hour. When I came across questions like that I always wanted to write in *Why doesn't he just take a plane, like normal people?* The coolest thing about Noah was that, unlike 99.999 percent of the universe, he was actually interested in my answers to the questions. It didn't feel like he was asking them because the SAT Saviors Handbook for Tutors said he had to. In fact, he made it so easy to talk about myself that it was next to impossible for me to get the scoop on him. Like what sign he was, what bands he liked, whether he thought a six-year age difference was that big a deal—that kind of stuff. I happen to be an Aquarian, which means I'm very independent and march to the beat of my own drum. I just hoped he wasn't a Cancer; if so, the relationship was doomed because they like to stay home all the time while we Aquarians like to travel to exotic locales, like New York City.

The most I was able to get out of him was that he was twenty-three (so I was a year off), had graduated from UC Berkeley two years earlier with a degree in English, and, in addition to being a writer who had come thisclose to getting published in Dave Eggers's magazine *The Believer* last year, was also a TA/caterer/tutor/dog walker. And that he grew up outside of Chicago and both his parents were psychoanalysts (*free therapy for the rest of my life!* I thought to myself).

The more we talked, the more I realized that Noah was an honest-to-goodness *adult*. A real man in every sense of the word, which, at fifteen and a half, was what I needed. As cute and potentially nice as Adam Silver may have been, he was still a *boy*—which meant that sooner or later I'd end up getting sick of him due to the fact that I was so mature for my age.

Finally Noah looked at his watch while I looked at the way the light hit the downy hairs on his wrist and thought of how nice his ring finger would look with a platinum band.

"Well, I guess that's it for today," I heard him say.

"It is?" I said. You'd think he had just told me I was too short to ride the Cyclone at Magic Mountain.

He laughed. "I think you're the first student I've had who actually looked disappointed that a session was over."

Yet again I blushed (maybe it was a medical condition?) and tried to think of something witty to say, but instead just let out a lort, which is a combination laugh/ snort.

"So would Thursdays at four and Saturdays at ten work for you?" he asked.

I nodded. I'd make any day work for me. I'd drop out of school if I had to.

"I was thinking maybe we could meet across the street at Café du Village next time," he said. He leaned in and whispered. "I try to stay away from Starbucks. Not a lot of . . . character. Know what I mean?"

I nodded. "Totally. And I *love* Café du Village." Actually, it was Malcolm who loved Café du Village. I tolerated it. Everyone who worked there was somehow related to the French owner either by birth or marriage—many of them straight off an Air France flight with little to no English skills. Because they had the nerve to get all pissy when anyone tried to order in English, it tended to put a damper on the dining experience. But, at that point, if Noah had suggested we meet at the Target snack bar, I would have agreed.

Outside, after he pulled me out of the way of a passing skateboarder (older men are so chivalrous!), he stuck out his hand. As I shook it I was pleased to find that it was moisturized and callus-free. "Well, it was nice to meet you, Cindy Gold." He smiled. "Till Thursday, then," he said.

"Hey, do you know that band 'Til Tuesday?" I asked, trying to make conversation because I wasn't ready to let go of his hand.

"Yeah," he said, impressed. "That was the band Aimee Mann was in during the eighties. You know their stuff?"

I nodded. "I'm a huge Aimee fan." I used my free hand to curl a curl around my finger and hoped I looked sexy. "In fact," I said, "I once saw her at Whole Foods and we had a conversation." This seemed to impress him even more. But I knew in my heart of hearts that a relationship built on half-truths wasn't much of a relationship, so I came clean. "Well, I mean, I said, 'Oh my God, I'm *so* sorry' after I bumped into her and made her drop her salad container and she said, 'No problem.'" I stepped out of the way to allow a gay couple and their Chinese baby girl by. "And, uh, that was kind of it."

He laughed. "Well, you still talked to her."

I loved that he looked on the bright side of things.

"Yeah, I guess." I still wasn't ready to let go.

"Well, Cindy"—he smiled—"I should get going. Have a great week."

"You, too," I replied, finally giving him his hand back.

As I watched him walk away, I thought about how you just never knew what the Universe had in store for you. Just the night before I had been ready to pack up and hitchhike to Guam, and then, without any warning, *boom*— I was madly in love. I whipped out my cell to call India. With only four days and four hours to turn myself into a walking, talking girl, I had some serious work to do.

chapter six

Being in love takes up a lot of energy. You spend all of your time thinking about the person, and all the Kodak moments that are going to happen between the two of you, and overanalyzing every stupid thing you said the last time you were together. With all that thinking going on, there's very little energy left to do anything physical. Like ride your bike home. Which means you have to walk it. Which, if you're on the phone, is probably a good thing.

"So how was it?" asked India when she answered the phone.

"Well, let's just say a Code Pink situation has arisen," I said into my hands-free mike.

"You met a guy?!" she squealed, as sitar music twanged in the background.

A Code Pink was anything that had to do with an as-yet-unrequited crush.

"Yup," I screamed into the mike.

"Ouch. Well, tell, tell!" she demanded. "Where'd you meet him?"

"Starbucks," I yelled.

"Are you hands-free?"

"Yeah," I shouted.

"I keep telling you, you don't have to *yell* when you do that."

"Sorry," I said in my normal voice, which was still on the loud side.

"Okay, so Starbucks? Cin, what were you thinking?!" India hated Starbucks, too.

However, her beef was more along the lines of them trying to pass themselves off as being "for the people" when they're just another huge corporation trying to screw the worker (or in this case, the Buckies) by barely paying them minimum wage.

"It wasn't my choice. It was a tutoring session."

"Wait a second—you're in like with your *tutor*?!" India squealed. Squealing was so not an India thing to do, but since me meeting a guy only occurred, oh, close to *never*, I guess it was understandable. "Omigod. How old is he?"

"Twenty-three," I whispered into the phone. I had no idea *why* I was whispering—there was no one near me other than the gardeners I kept passing.

"Omigod. We have to get Malcolm on the phone. Just

hold on, I'm going to conference him in," said India.

As I passed two dark-haired nannies, each pushing strollers with blond-haired, blue-eyed babies, I smiled at them, but they looked the other way. I don't know why people are always saying that L.A.'s such a friendly place—frankly, I think it's the exact opposite. I wondered where Noah stood on the whole nanny thing. With both of us writing at home, I didn't think we'd need one.

The phone clicked. "An older man, *chica*?!" said Malcolm. "How *Lost in Translation* of you!" he squealed. *Lost in Translation* was one of the few movies of this millennium that Malcolm thought had any value.

"Ewww!" India and I squealed back.

"Bill Murray's, like, in his sixties," I said. "Noah's only twenty-three. Hey, that's not *too* old for me, is it?"

"Of course not," said Malcolm. I could hear Madonna's "Material Girl" thumping away in his room. "Someone as wise and mature as you *needs* an older man. Otherwise you'd get bored of him," he assured me.

"Wait a second," piped in India. "*I'm* wise and mature, too, but you keep trying to convince me to go out with that guy who works at the Skate Shop and he's six months younger than me."

"That's because he looks like Brad Pitt. And the whole older woman/younger man thing works, too. Just look at Madonna and Guy—she's ten years older than him," he replied.

"But what about Adam?" India asked.

"Who?" I replied.

"Adam Silver? The guy you've been obsessed with for—I don't know—*ever*?"

"Yeah, we broke up. I mean, Adam's great and all, and he'll always occupy a special place in my heart, but, you guys, Noah's my *soul mate*."

"Yesterday afternoon you were positive that Adam was your soul mate," countered Malcolm.

"But Noah's my soul-mate soul mate," I replied. "I'm telling you—this is the real thing."

"Okay, so if this was a movie, who would play him?" asked Malcolm.

"Zach Braff."

"Nice," said India.

"Is that Zach Braff pre-*Garden State* or post-Mandy Moore? Because I have to say I think some of his hotness has been diluted post-Mandy."

"Post-*Garden State,* prebreakup," I replied.

"Okay, good," said Malcolm. "And you're lucky he's already out of high school—less of a chance he'll be freaked out by The Letter."

"He *did* seem to like activists," I screamed over the siren of a passing police car, and paused to redo my ponytail, which, as part of the curse of having thick frizzy hair, had fallen apart a few blocks earlier. Holding my bike with one hand, I used the other to wipe the sweat from my neck on the leg of my jeans, which were sticking to me. The haze of June Gloom had burned off and it was about twenty degrees warmer than it had been when I left the house. Walking my bike was proving to be just as exhausting as riding it.

"Listen, I can barely hear you, plus Code Pinks can't really be dealt with over the phone. I say we meet at Mani's at O-1600 to come up with a game plan." "Mani's" was Mani's Bakery, which India liked because everything there was fruit-juice sweetened.

"Huh?" said India.

"That's two o'clock," I said.

"Look at you all math-wise," said India. "He must be a very good tutor."

"Actually, sixteen hundred hours is four o'clock," said Malcolm.

"Oh," I said. "Whoops."

"We're supposed to have family meditation time then," said India.

"India, you can get enlightened any day. But Cindy meeting a guy—an *older* man—this is big," said Malcolm. "Especially when her chances of anyone at Castle Heights asking her out because of The Letter are, like, zilch."

"Gee, thanks, Malcolm," I said.

"So I'll see you ladies there?" he asked.

"Yup," I coughed through the exhaust fumes of a moving van that almost hit me.

"Adieu," said Malcolm.

"*Namaste*," said India, which means, "The teacher in me bows to the teacher in you," or something corny like that. It's the way all yoga people say hello and good-bye to each other.

"Bye," I said, and closed my phone.

Figuring I should work on getting some muscle tone, I got on my bike and rode the rest of the way home. As I mentally went through all my closets and drawers, I realized I owned nothing even remotely girly to wear to our Thursday tutoring session.

I was glad to see my dad's Mercedes in the driveway. Well, part of it, at least. Most of it was dwarfed by the huge fountain in our front yard. All of the other houses in our neighborhood are landscaped with beautiful flowers and plants, but in keeping with the Zen motif, all we have is the fountain, which makes a ton of noise. My dad had gone ballistic when he found out how much it cost (something like $10,000 because it had been imported from a monastery in Tibet), but he caved when Clarissa told him that the garden designer had said it would bring harmony to a blended family.

When I got inside, I found my dad and Spencer on the couch in the family room watching golf, with their eyes glazed over and dumb smiles on their faces. They looked almost identical, except that Spencer was wearing a diaper and drooling.

I put Spencer on my lap as I sank into the couch next to my dad.

"Hi, Monkey Girl," my dad said without looking away from the television.

My dad thought the fact that I looked like a baby chimp when I was born was "cute." I thought it was horrifying. I reached into the bag of tortilla chips on his lap. "(A) We decided I was too old for you to keep calling me that, (B) you're not allowed to eat chips in the family room, and (C) you're not supposed to be eating these, period, because of your gallbladder," I said as I crunched away. *I* didn't have a gallbladder problem.

"(A) I've been calling you that since the day you were born, and (B) and (C) don't tell and don't tell," he said as he shoved more chips into his mouth, giving one here and there to Spencer.

I took the bag away from him and put it on the floor. "I'm serious, Dad. You've got to take care of yourself." In just the last year, my dad had had two heart-attack scares. Both, thank God, turned out to be indigestion.

He was too busy watching some blond guy putt to notice the bag was gone. After the little ball went into the even smaller hole, he clicked the television off with the remote and turned to me.

"So, sweetie, how are you?" he asked.

"I'm good," I replied, brushing crumbs off his shirt so Clarissa wouldn't know he had been cheating on the almost-nothing-but-water-and-lettuce diet she had put him on to get rid of the small beach ball that doubled as his stomach.

"Where've you been?"

"At tutoring," I said. *Falling madly in love,* I thought as I snuggled Spencer to my chest. He immediately grabbed for my necklace. The minute Spencer saw something shiny, he grabbed for it. A true L.A. kid.

"How's it going with that kid with the band? What was his name? Achmed?"

"Ahmet. It's not. Remember Clarissa fired him?"

"Right. I forgot."

"This one's name is Noah," I said. *Your future son-in-law.*

Spencer cooed loudly and smiled. Maybe he was psychic like India's mom's friend Sola.

"Now, what's this Clarissa was telling me about an editorial you wrote for the school paper?" he asked.

"It wasn't an editorial. It was a letter to the editor."

"Well, from what she told me, it was pretty harsh. Can I see it?"

I ran upstairs to get a copy and brought it back downstairs. As he read it, I counted three *hmm*s, two sighs, and a lort (it was hereditary), but since my dad had honed his poker face in a monthly game with a bunch of old TV action stars from the eighties, it was hard to tell what he thought about it.

When he was done he handed it back to me.

"So what do you think?" I asked nervously.

"What do I think? I think it's . . . fantastic!" he boomed.

Not used to seeing so much emotion from my father, Spencer began to clap his hands, which made us both laugh.

"Really?"

"Really. I'm very proud of you, honey. It took a lot of guts to write something like that."

"You don't think I can get sued for slander or anything, do you?"

He laughed. "No, I think you're okay. But if you do, I'll serve as your legal counsel at a very reduced rate." He hugged me. "It's great. Very impassioned."

"Thanks," I said. "Unfortunately it didn't go over so well, though. It pissed a lot of people off."

"That doesn't surprise me." He sighed. "Sometimes when you touch a nerve, people get angry. Especially if you're calling into question the very ideals that they've based their identity upon," he explained. As he said that, I felt like I got a glimpse of the ACLU lawyer my dad used to be before he gave it up to go work at the New York office of the studio so that I'd have my own bedroom in the burbs rather than have to sleep in a drawer in their fifth-floor Greenwich Village walk-up. It was like listening to a balding, middle-aged Jewish Obi-Wan Kenobi.

"Yeah, well, now everyone at school basically hates me," I said.

"Hey, when you're a radical, you just have to roll with the punches. Look at Gloria Steinem—you think she had an easy time of it at the beginning? I remember being at a pro-choice rally during law school and people were throwing eggs at her."

"Dad?"

"What?" he asked, reaching for the bag of chips again. Because he was being so supportive, I decided to let it slide.

"Mom used to write a lot of letters to the editor, too, didn't she?" I asked quietly. We never talked about my mom.

The mention of her name made him squirm, but it also made his face soften. "Yeah, she sure did," he replied.

I thought he was going to say something else, but just then the front door opened and the Clones flip-flopped in, carrying what sounded like a truckload of shopping bags. I have to admit, he looked relieved that our conversation was cut short, which wasn't surprising seeing that his grief over Mom's death ended up manifesting in workaholism and an almost pathological aversion to communicating on a deep, soulful level. At least that's what Dr. Greenburg said.

"I *so* saw those Christian Louboutins first!" said Britney. "And I'm wearing them to the prom. You can wear the Guccis."

As Clarissa had promised them each a pair of

designer shoes for the prom, they had bought and returned countless pairs over the last month in their quest to find the perfect pair.

"You did not!" Ashley retorted. "And they're too high for you anyway—you know you can't walk in stilettos."

"I can so!" said Ashley.

"Fine. Well, then I'm going to Neiman's next week and getting those Pradas," said Ashley as the two of them barreled into the family room carrying handfuls of shoe-box-stuffed shopping bags. "Where's Mom?" they demanded in unison.

"Hello, Britney, hello, Ashley, how is your day going so far?" my dad asked pleasantly.

"Horrible," said Britney. "Mom's still not back from Botoxing?" she asked.

"She's on her way. So why horrible?" he said.

"Because we just ran into Dakota Greene at Saks and she told us that *she's* going to be wearing a Jaden, too, which is, like, *totally* uncool," explained Ashley.

My dad was confused. "What's a Jaden and why is it uncool?" he asked.

Britney sighed at his ignorance. "It's uncool because Dakota is the biggest hoochie in the senior class." A hoochie with a millionaire father, that is.

"'Hoochie'?" he asked. It was weird to see my dad looking so lost. Usually he had a killer I'll-sue-you-for-all-you're-worth attitude.

"Hoodrat," I said by way of explanation.

Still nothing.

"Slut," the three of us said in unison.

He turned red. "Oh."

"C'mon, Ash, I want to call Stefani and see if she's heard if anyone *else* is going to be wearing a Jaden," said Britney. "We might as well just wear something from Old Navy," she grumbled as they left the room.

"I still don't know what a Jaden is," my dad said after they left.

"Jaden's the designer who's going to make their prom dresses," I said as I took the bag of chips away from a now-naked Spencer.

"I thought they already *had* dresses," he said. "I remember hitting the roof about the credit card bill."

"They do," I said.

"Remind me who they're going with again?" he asked.

"Ashley's going with Wally Lieberstein and Britney's going with Conrad SanFilippo." Wally was the son of the guy who invented the computer code for that feature on Amazon.com that says "If you liked *Harry Potter and the Sorcerer's Stone*, then you'll really like *Lord of the Rings*," which netted him like a gazillion dollars and a French château-looking monstrosity in Bel Air. At seventeen, Wally's hairline had almost entirely receded, but he was a really nice guy. Sort of on the nerdier side of seminerd. And Conrad's father was a real-estate developer responsible for The Canyon, a big mall that had opened the year before a mile away from another mall called The Grove. Conrad wasn't a seminerd—he was just creepy, like he belonged on *The Sopranos*.

It may seem weird that two girls as cute and popular as the Clones would end up having to go to the prom with guys like that, but like all of L.A, Castle Heights was just *filled* with gorgeous people. In fact, they had done away with "Best Looking" in our yearbook because everyone was so beautiful. And while Wally and Conrad may not have been hotties, they are definitely two of the richest kids at Castle Heights, which in some eyes (I'm not going to name names here) is just as good, if not better.

The front door opened again. "Hellloooo! I'm hooome!" trilled Clarissa. I shoved the bag of chips underneath the couch while my dad brushed away any stray crumbs.

"Hi, honey. We're in the family room," shouted my dad.

Clarissa came in looking even more expressionless than usual and gave my dad and Spencer real kisses and me an air kiss. "Warren, honey, you know I'm not thrilled about people sitting in here," she said.

"Clarissa, it's called a *family* room," he replied.

"I know that, sweetie, but you also have a TV in your study," she purred as she started massaging his shoulders. In keeping with the Zen look, my dad's "study" had been stripped of all furniture save for a desk, a chair, and a big-screen television. Clarissa's eyes swept over the coffee table as she checked for rings from any coasterless glasses. "Cindy Ella, honey, how are you feeling? Are you done acting out?"

"Who's acting out? You're acting out?" my dad asked anxiously.

"*No.* It's just that this morning—"

"Honey, can you do my neck?" he asked Clarissa.

"Of course, angel. Cindy Ella, you and Spencer move so I can massage your daddy's neck real good," she said.

Spencer and I plopped down in the overstuffed chair across from the couch. You had to hand it to Clarissa—she always went full out, so the chair was just as comfortable as the couch. She might value prom dresses over higher education, but I will admit that she treats my dad like a king. Retro, maybe, but it works for them. She dressed him in nice clothes (left to his own devices, he still favored ACLU-wear, like corduroy jackets with suede elbow patches); she got them into a good country club; she made sure they socialized with other couples that lived in Zen motif houses. I once overheard him telling my aunt Rhoda that you only get one love of your life and my mom had been it, but that Clarissa made a great "second wife." Not exactly the kind of romance I hope to find when I grow up, but maybe it's because he's a lawyer rather than a passionate artistic type like me.

"So did the girls get home from Saks yet?" asked Clarissa as she massaged away.

"Yes," said my dad. "With a dozen shoe boxes each. Clarissa, I thought we decided you were going to take back those credit cards . . . "

"Honey, I *am*," she cooed as she massaged harder. "Right after the prom. But there's so much to do to get ready that I can't possibly get it done all by myself," she added as she leaned forward and kissed the bald spot on his head. "Now take your sneakers off and I'll do your feet."

My dad took off his sneakers and reorganized himself on the couch while Clarissa got to work.

He sighed happily. Next to a juicy lawsuit, my dad loved nothing more than a good foot rub and back scratch. "What are they planning to do?" he asked. "Change their shoes after every song?"

"No, silly! They're just being prepared. Once they try them with their new dresses, they'll decide on one pair and the rest will go back."

He turned around and gave her a doubtful look.

"I swear!" she promised.

Like most women, Clarissa and the Clones loved shoes. I, however, had been absent the day they handed out that chromosome. The one time I tried on a pair of heels at Nordstrom's, I fell and twisted my ankle and brought the shoe salesman down with me, which is why I stick to Uggs for fall and winter, J.Crew flip-flops for spring and summer, and a pair of all-season pink suede

Birkenstock rip-offs that I got at Target. Boring, I know, but much safer for anyone who might be within twenty-five feet of me.

"What is that on the baby's face?" asked Clarissa, leaning forward to squint Botox-style at Spencer. I could see that she was about to start one of her speeches about not eating outside of the kitchen, so I set him on the floor and stood up.

"India's picking me up in a few minutes and we're going to meet Malcolm at Mani's, okay?" I said over my shoulder.

"Sure," said my dad.

"But don't forget we have that dinner dance at the country club, so I need you home by six. Okay, honey?" she called after me.

"Okay," I yelled back as I ran up the stairs to change my clothes and wash off the grime from my bike ride. Clarissa may be obsessed with the fact that I don't have a lot of friends (not to mention a boyfriend), but at least my lack of a social life affords her a built-in babysitter.

Clean-faced and minty-breathed, I passed by Ashley's Shabby Chic'd bedroom, where she and Britney were busy shoving their feet into various pointy-toed stilettos. I wish I'd had a camera. The pained grimaces on their faces would have made a great antiprom PSA.

"Cindy, c'mere for a second," Britney yelled out.

I walked over to the doorway and tried to locate them

in the sea of shoes, tank tops, and jeans littering the floor. Despite Evelin's constant attempts to restore order, their rooms always looked like Bloomingdale's dressing rooms after a three-day sale. Plus, the overdone floral motif made me want to start sneezing. "What?" I asked.

"You didn't happen to hear who Adam Silver asked to the prom, did you?" Ashley said as she traded a slingback for a mule.

Just the sheer mention of his name made me feel like I had stuck my finger in a light socket. "Uh, no. Who?" I asked.

"We don't know," said Britney as she yanked a pump off and jammed her foot into a strappy sandal, which, from the look on her face, was about two sizes too small. "Ouch. That's why we're asking. We thought maybe Malcolm had heard."

Ashley tottered over to the full-length mirror to check herself out. "I still say he's going with Hilary Duff and it's just that her publicist made him swear up and down on a stack of Bibles that he'd keep it quiet so the paparazzi don't show up."

Britney joined Ashley at the mirror. In their matching jeans and tanks (Ashley's was pink, Britney's was red), they looked like a taller, less trashy Olsen/Hilton sisters hybrid.

"Maybe he's that other senior who's not going," I said, trying to keep any hint of hope out of my voice. I knew it shouldn't matter now that I had Noah, but I still didn't want to think about Adam Silver slow-dancing to some John Mayer song with another girl.

They both turned to me and stared with disbelief. You'd think Sushi had just spoken. "Are. You. *Crazy?*" said Ashley.

I shrugged. "Maybe he read my letter and wants to set a good example for his two younger sisters." Dr. Greenburg and I had spent a lot of time discussing what he liked to call my "propensity for magical thinking." As far as I was concerned, it was more "the power of intention," which I had once heard this guy Dr. Wayne Dyer talking about during the PBS pledge drive as I was flipping to The N to watch *Degrassi*.

"Enough with the letter!" said Ashley. "Of *course* he's going. He's, like, the most popular guy in all of California."

Britney sighed and staggered over to me in her unmatching shoes and put her hands on my shoulders. "Cindy?" she said with a concerned look on her face.

"Yeah?" I said warily.

"Did the fact that everyone thinks you're a total freak because of your letter not teach you anything?" she asked, genuinely puzzled.

Ashley came over and joined us. "Don't you just want to be *normal?*" she said earnestly.

"Meaning . . . ?"

"Like us!" Britney replied.

"Um . . . " Thankfully, before I was forced to carefully word my response, I was saved by Goldie Hawn's beep. "Shoot. There's India. Can we talk about this later?"

Luckily they had already gone back to admiring their feet and ignored me. But now I couldn't stop thinking about Adam Silver.

"Stop it," I whispered as I ran down the stairs. "Adam is your *past*—you have Noah now."

I'd be darned if I was going to turn into one of those drama queens who sits there whining about how she's torn between two men.

chapter seven

It turned out that being in love not only took up a lot of energy—it also made you really hungry.

"Tell me what it's like . . . is it just incredible?" asked India dreamily as we sat at a table shoved against the wall at Mani's. As usual, the restaurant was packed with kids (it was cheap), City Yoga students (it was healthy), and Fred Segal shoppers (again, the cheap factor—after you've just spent fifty dollars on a T-shirt that intentionally looks old and faded, you don't have a lot left over for lunch).

"Being in love?" I asked with my mouth full.

"No! The turkey burger!" she replied. India was obsessed with non-soy-based protein the way the Clones were obsessed with shoes.

"Oh," I said after swallowing. "Yeah. It's amazing." I held it out toward her. "Want some?"

She gave me a dirty look and went back to picking at her carob cookie. I found the idea of fake chocolate a total psych-out, but I had to admit that being vegan since birth definitely gave you great skin. India's was what old-fashioned English novelists would call "alabaster." If real life were a movie, Kate Hudson would play her. Despite the fact that she refused to shave her armpits and liked to wear overalls and bandannas (like she was today), boys thought she was hot. What was funny was that India couldn't care less. She was more interested in spending her time studying so she could get into Stanford, rather than join the Peace Corps like her parents were pressuring her to do.

The noise level inside the restaurant was deafening, with everyone trying to outgossip one another about the latest celebrity hookup or rehab visit, but Malcolm was focused on his *Us Weekly* (a.k.a. the Bible). Finally, after India threw a couple of my fries at him, he looked up.

"Why oh why was the Good Lord so cruel as to make Jake Gyllenhaal straight?" He sighed as he took off his reading glasses—the ones that make him look like a young Denzel Washington. Even though it was Saturday (read: casual attire permitted), he was still wearing his standard uniform of pressed khakis, a starched white oxford, and loafers. In the winter he sometimes added a sweater vest. It sounds geeky, but being fabulous and gay, Malcolm pulled it off and made it look nerd chic rather than preppy loser.

"Okay, dolls, let's get down to business. Cindy, tell us

everything you know about The Tutor so far," he demanded.

I wiped my mouth and pushed my plate away. "Well, he went to Berkeley—"

India nodded approvingly. "A liberal. Good. Did he happen to mention what protests he took part in?"

"We haven't gotten that personal yet," I said. "And he's a writer."

Malcolm gasped. "Ooh! Maybe he'll give me notes on my script."

"He's a novelist."

"Then why's he living in L.A.?" asked Malcolm, puzzled.

"Good question," I answered.

I shared the rest of my limited knowledge about Noah (which took five seconds) and was relieved when the two of them signed off on him becoming my newest (more like my first) boyfriend.

"Okay, now comes the hard part—getting him to see you not just as one of his students, but as a potential life partner," said Malcolm as he took out a notepad and a pen. "Which is why we'll need to come up with *Operation Turn Cindy into a Girl*. First we'll have to decide on a look . . . I'm thinking maybe Molly circa *Pretty in Pink*. But then again, that whole tailored thing she had going in *Breakfast Club* was smart, too—"

"She only wore one outfit in that," India said. "The whole movie took place over one day."

"Thank you, Ms. Logic Police. However, it happened to be a *very* nice outfit," said Malcolm. "Don't you remember those fabulous boots she had?"

"I already have a pair of boots," I piped up. "My Uggs. But it's too hot to wear them." I sighed. "Remember, the last time I wore them was that day in January when I passed Adam Silver in the hall and our shoulders almost touched."

"I remember," said India. "You talked about it for weeks."

"You guys, I have to tell you, this is really freaking me out," I admitted.

"We're just talking about some wardrobe adjustments here," huffed Malcolm. "It's not like I'm suggesting you get a boob job or anything."

"No, I mean one minute I'm totally into Noah, and then the next all these music videos of me and Adam Silver are running on my brain screen. It's like I'm schizophrenic or something."

Malcolm reached for my hand. "Cindy, it's time to let Adam go. The truth of the matter is that seeing that you're so mature, you *need* to be with an older man."

"Yeah, otherwise you'll just end up keeping yourself small in order to make sure he's not intimidated, and then, one day when you're in your forties, you'll realize you totally wasted the best years of your life and leave in the middle of the night and go live in a commune in Oregon like my aunt Betsy did," said India.

As difficult as my abandonment complex made it to let go of things, I knew that my friends were right. If this had a chance of working, I couldn't just give Noah part of my heart—I needed to give him *all* of it.

Just then a group of guys walked through the door. Actually, it was more like they "rolled through" like you see in rap videos, so the fact that they were all white made them look ridiculous. "Oh no," I said, turning away to face the wall.

India and Malcolm turned around to look. "Ew. What is *that*?" India asked.

"And would someone please tell them the whole 'jeans twenty sizes too big' thing ended five years ago?" added Malcolm.

"See the pudgy one with the HIP-HOP HEEB T-shirt?" I said to the wall. "That's Michael Rosenberg." I prayed to God he didn't come over to our table.

"He's coming over to our table," announced India.

"'Sup yo!" I heard him say a moment later.

I turned around and tried to look semipleased to see him. "Hey, Michael. What's up?"

"Nothing. Just chillin' after Fred Segal. I just got this," he said, pointing to his T-shirt. "Ain't it the shizzle, yo?" he asked. Could he not see that Malcolm was African-American and therefore might be offended by the way he was talking? Sure, Malcolm was the preppiest black kid around, plus he was gay, but Michael didn't know that.

"Um . . . I guess so?" I said/asked.

"So what's up with that letter you wrote in your school paper?" he bellowed. "Your moms called mine to see if I'd ask you to the prom because no one will come near you now." I had forgotten what a loud talker Michael was.

The girls at the table next to us stopped talking about the latest celebrity sex tape making the Internet rounds and turned to look at me. From their tight T-shirts and miniskirts that barely covered their you-know-whats, I was pretty sure they went to Immaculate Heart, the all-girls Catholic school just east of Hollywood, in Los Feliz.

"Do you think you could lower your voice, please?" I whispered. I didn't need every teenager in L.A. knowing my business.

"But I've already got a date," he went on in an equally loud voice. "So I couldn't even ask you if I wanted to. Not that I'd want to. Check it—I'm done with Jewish girls."

"What's wrong with Jewish girls?" asked India defensively. Even though she was raised without any religion other than the "Divine within," her father had been brought up a conservative Jew. And one of her pet peeves was when people made sweeping generalizations about anything—whether it be religion or reality television.

"Yo, chill, babe," Michael said, raising his arms to ward off the hostility that was oozing out of her. The bottom of his T-shirt crept up, exposing his pasty belly. My appetite suddenly gone, I pushed away the rest of my fries.

"'Babe'?" said India as loudly as Michael.

I could tell things were about to head into dangerous territory, as India's other pet peeve was being called "babe" or "miss" or any other overtly feminine term. "Listen, Michael, we're kind of in the middle of something," I said.

"That's cool, that's cool" He nodded. "Check you lata," he said as he rolled away.

"I can't believe you went out with that guy," India said.

"Don't remind me," I moaned. "I can't believe Clarissa actually called his mom. That's beyond mortifying. I'll be so glad when this stupid prom is over."

India and Malcolm exchanged guilty looks.

"What?" I said as I started back in on the fries.

Malcolm shook his head. "You know, if anyone saw the way you ate, they'd definitely think you were a purger."

I shrugged. "I keep telling you—it's my fast metabolism. Plus, I could never make myself throw up. I'm way too lazy. But don't think I can't tell you're trying to change the subject. What is it?"

"Well, we were going to wait until later to tell you, so we wouldn't ruin your first day of being in love, but I guess now's as good a time as ever," Malcolm said.

"What?" I asked again, jamming the fries in my mouth double time. I could tell whatever it was wasn't good.

"Um, well, I kind of have a confession to make."

"Yeah, I figured that part out. So what is it?"

He looked over at India, who gave him an encouraging nod.

"I'm going," he announced.

"Going where?" I said.

"To the prom," he replied.

"What?! How? Why?" I asked, dumbfounded.

"You forgot 'when' and 'who,'" said India, the A-plus student.

He shrugged. "Because I was asked?"

"But who are you going with?" I managed to get out.

"Colin Fisher."

I gasped. "Colin Fisher asked you to the prom? Wow." For a moment I forgot my antiprom stance and allowed myself to be duly impressed. Adam Silver may have been the cutest boy at Castle Heights, but Colin Fisher was definitely the coolest. In fact, he had been one of the first people in the country to get an iPhone.

I could feel my abandonment complex starting to rear its head. I turned to India. "Please tell me you're not going, too," I pleaded.

She patted my hand. "Of course not."

"Thank God."

India gave me a dirty look.

"I mean thank Goddess," I said, and turned back to Malcolm. "So when did all this happen?"

"We ran into him and Justin Starobin at the movies last night and India asked them to sit with us and—ready for this?—it turns out that Colin loves to put Junior Mints in his popcorn, too! So, of course, we bonded over that because what are the chances of someone else in the world liking something like that, let alone someone in the city of Los Angeles—"

"If I ate sugar, I'd bet *I'd* like the taste of Junior Mints with popcorn," India piped up.

"Okay: (A) you *don't* eat sugar, and (B) you're a girl, so even if you were gay, I'd still never want to date you," Malcolm shot back. He took my hand. "Look, Cin, we all know how you feel about the prom, and I love you like a sister, even though any sister of mine would *have* to have a little more fashion sense, but the more I think about it—I really want to go to the prom."

"But we're only sophomores," I reminded him. "You still have two more chances to go. Who knows," I said excitedly. "Maybe people will have a delayed reaction to The Letter and next year's prom won't be about dresses, or shoes, or prom queens."

Malcolm rolled his eyes as he pointed at my OCCUPATION: REALITY AVOIDANCE T-shirt. "You're definitely wearing the right T-shirt today," he said.

"Seriously. Maybe next year it'll be about what it was always *supposed* to be about."

"And that would be . . . ?" asked Malcolm.

"Like I said in my letter: a rite of passage into early adulthood."

"Yeah, right," said Malcolm. "And in *that* movie, I'll get to go with Jake Gyllenhaal."

"Cin, are those *your* words, or that Naomi woman's?" asked India.

"They're my words," I said indignantly. "I mean, she may have said something similar on TV that night, but I felt that way before I saw her."

"Well, I've been dying for Colin to ask me out all year," said Malcolm.

"Yeah, I know you have." I sighed.

"So are you okay with this or are you going to secretly hate me for the rest of our lives?" he asked.

"I guess I'm okay with you going," I replied. "But unfortunately I don't think I'll be able to help you get ready or any of that kind of stuff."

He squeezed my hand. "Of course. I know you have a reputation to uphold. Plus the lack-of-fashion-sense thing wouldn't really be much of a help anyway." He flopped back in his chair. "Thank God *that's* over with."

Another dirty look from India.

"God, Goddess—whatever. Oy, I feel so much better now that we've talked about this. I was afraid it might turn into a whole Paris/Nicole thing." He sat up and rubbed his hands together. "Now let's get back to *Operation Turn Cindy into a Girl*."

Over the next hour, we came up with the following game plan:

1. Field trip to The Grove to load up on staples that will transmit to Noah the message that I am, indeed, a girl, i.e., flouncy skirts to show off my "coltish" legs (Malcolm's word, not mine), V-neck T-shirts to showcase my nonexistent cleavage, Victoria's Secret Wonderbra to *give* me some cleavage. (Note to self: check to see if WonderBras even come in size 34AA.)

2. Make appointment with Clarissa's hair guru, Astrid, to have three inches of split ends cut off and highlights applied.

3. Rent every Molly Ringwald and Sandra Bullock movie ever made to study how they act around guys.

4. Retire previous solemn oath to never wear makeup.

5. Go to Sephora and purchase makeup (including nonglitter nail polish to put on bitten fingernails).

6. Be myself. Or, to be more precise, be whoever I find "myself" to be after completing steps 1–5.

By the time India dropped me off at home, I felt nauseous, partly because she was a horrible driver (she had only passed her driving test because the DMV guy felt sorry for her since it was her third try) and partly because the idea of morphing myself into someone else just to get a guy to like me seemed so . . . *wrong.*

"Look, it's not like anyone's asking you to *change*," said India over the roar of Goldie Hawn's engine as we sat in my driveway. She was afraid to turn the ignition off, for fear it wouldn't start again. "All we're asking is that you play up what's already there. You know, if you tried, you could be a total Babezilla."

I rolled my eyes. "Oh, please."

"You could!"

"Well, I'm not interested in going out with someone who's looking for a 'Babezilla,'" I said as I got out of the car. "I want someone who loves me for my mind. Like Noah does."

"He's still a guy."

"A girl can dream, can't she?" I said as I slammed the door. "I'll call you later."

I walked in the front door to find a naked Spencer decorating Sushi with Post-it notes. He looked up at me and cooed, holding out his arms for a hug.

"Hey, my little nudist friend," I said as I picked him up. "What's going on, *muchacho?*"

As he burped in response, Clarissa came click-clacking down the stairs, dressed in a fuchsia dress and stiletto heels that looked more appropriate for a nightclub than a country club. "Oh, good. You're home. Unfortunately I didn't have a chance to give Spencer his dinner," she said.

"But I think there's some kung pao tofu in the freezer if you want to defrost it."

At the sound of the word *tofu*, Spencer's fat cheeks began to scrunch up into a premeltdown expression. "Don't worry," I whispered into his ear. "No tofu, I promise."

"What was that, sugar?" asked Clarissa as she applied another coat of lipstick in front of the hall mirror.

Out came Spencer's three-toothed smile.

"Nothing. Hey, Clarissa, I was wondering . . . do you have any extra makeup that you don't use?" I asked.

She turned to me. "Why?"

I thought about lying and saying it was for a battered women's shelter or something equally do-goody, but I figured I needed all the good karma I could get if I was serious about winning Noah's heart. "Well, I was thinking I might do some . . . experimenting tonight," I said. "You know, just play around."

Clarissa gasped. "You mean . . . you're finally willing to wear some makeup?!"

I shrugged.

She rushed over and hugged me. "Oh, Cindy Ella," she said. "I kept telling your father I knew this day would finally come!" Before an allergy attack from her giant cloud of perfume started, she let me go.

"Of course you can have some of my old makeup, sweetie! I'll be right back," she said as she tottered back up the stairs.

I put Spencer down so he could go terrorize Sushi, who was happily chomping on his foot in the corner, and heard what sounded like a minor earthquake going on above. Five minutes later Clarissa came down with a big plastic storage container filled to the gills with every imaginable cosmetic.

"Here," she said as she thrust it into my arms.

"Thanks," I gasped as I struggled to hold on to it.

"I just wish I could help you," she said. Was that a *genuine* smile on her face? "Maybe tomorrow, after you're done at the yoga studio, I'll give you a makeover."

"Um, okay," I said.

She pulled my head toward her and started moving it around as if it wasn't attached to my body, examining it from different angles. "We'll have so much fun! You know how I just *love* a challenge."

My dad came down the stairs fixing his tie. "What's going on?"

"Warren, Cindy Ella's finally becoming a woman! Isn't that wonderful?!"

The way his eyes narrowed made it clear that he didn't think it was so wonderful. "What are you talking about? She's not having sex, is she? You're not having sex, are you?" he asked me.

"No, Dad. I'm not having sex," I replied.

"Of course she's not having sex—she'd have to kiss a boy first for that to happen," Clarissa assured him. "What

I mean is that she's going to start wearing makeup."

"She's too young for makeup," my dad said.

"Oh, please. She is not—the twins started wearing it when they were fourteen," said Clarissa. "She's not going to wear a lot, honey," she purred as she fixed his tie. "Just some blush. And a little eye shadow. And, of course, a smudge of eyeliner. And maybe some lipstick—"

I was starting to itch. What had I gotten myself into?

"Maybe we can even do something about the bump on her nose," she murmured as she began to futz with his hair to try to cover up his bald spot.

"Well, I don't want her running around town looking like some underage Romanian model," my dad said, smoothing his hair back to its original style. Did parents not remember how maddening it was to be talked about like you weren't in the room?

"Don't worry—I won't," I piped up as they headed for the door. *I'll just wear it until Noah and I are officially a couple and then I'll return to my* au naturel *look,* I thought to myself.

Thankfully they left before Clarissa could scare my dad any more. I should've just gone the battered-women route—now she'd never leave me alone. Then again, who knew? Maybe it would be the beginning of a beautiful stepmother-daughter relationship.

After Spencer, Sushi, and I shared some frozen pad thai and Indian curry, I plopped Spencer down in front of

Elmopallooza and started hunting for "Makeup Application for Dummies" articles on the Web. As Spencer and I sang along with En Vogue to "I Want a Monster to Be My Friend," *wassup?* flashed in the upper right-hand corner of the screen.

AntiPrincess: nada. about to give myself a crash course in makeup. be very glad ur not a girl. what r u doing?
BklynBoy: getting ready to go to a party.

I looked at the clock. It was already ten in New York. People went out so late there. For someone like me who needed at least eight hours of sleep every night, I was going to have to take lots of naps when I lived there.

BklynBoy: u don't need makeup. ur hot w/o it!
AntiPrincess: o plz. @ least u know what i look like . . . when r u going to send me a pic?!!?

As usual he ignored me.

BklynBoy: so how's the anti-prom crusade coming along?

The truth was, with *Operation Turn Cindy into a Girl* now at the forefront of my mind, I had almost forgotten about the prom.

AntiPrincess: eh. not so good. everyone except for 2 sr's are going. and one's in a coma.

I stared at the cursor, wondering whether I should bring up Noah.

AntiPrincess: hey—i need some advice.

BklynBoy: 'bout what?

AntiPrincess: boys. i mean, men.

BklynBoy: men????

AntiPrincess: well, he's 23.

BklynBoy: a little old for u, don't u think?

AntiPrincess: hey mr. big sr—ur always saying how mature i am for a sophomore!

BklynBoy: true . . . who is he?

AntiPrincess: my SAT tutor.

BklynBoy: LOL!!!!!!!!! does he whisper sweet latin roots in ur ear?

AntiPrincess: ha ha. stop laughing. he's very cool. anyway, india & malcolm keep saying i have to make myself over & turn into some sort of jessica simpson wannabe but that's just so not moi . . .

BklynBoy: so don't. just be urself.

AntiPrincess: that's what i said . . . but they keep saying it's not enuf. i mean, i'm willing to MAYBE shake it up a little in the wardrobe dept., but that's about it. i'm not going to act all stepford-like.

BklynBoy: if this guy is worth it, he'll think ur smokin' just the way u r.

Elmo and the kids were finishing up their last song, which meant that once Spencer came out of his Muppet coma, all hell would break loose.

Antiprincess: thx. i should go put spence to bed. have fun 2nite.
BklynBoy: ciao.

As I gave Spencer his bath, I thought about how weird it was that you could become such good friends with someone you'd never actually met. Over the last year, BklynBoy had come to know as much about me as India and Malcolm did. He knew about Clarissa and the Clones, and how bummed out I still got around the anniversary of my mom's death, and how I missed the relationship me and my dad used to have when it was just the two of us and we'd do fun things like have D days, which meant we'd only eat foods that started with the letter *D* or watch movies that started with the letter *D* or sing songs that started . . . you get the picture. I had even sent him some of my poetry. India and Malcolm didn't even *know* I wrote poetry. It wasn't any good, but BklynBoy said I was like a female Bob Dylan, which coming from him was a huge compliment because Bob Dylan was his favorite singer of all time. I guess the anonymity of the Internet made it easier just to be yourself. That's why I didn't care about not knowing his name or whether he was rock-star cute. Obviously I hoped he wasn't some gross forty-five-year-old, but I didn't think he was. He was too up on all the latest bands.

After putting Spencer to bed, I went into Britney's room to grab some magazines. It was identical to Ashley's except the color motif was mauve rather than rose. Underneath all her size-four clothes were *Teen Vogue* and regular *Vogue* and *CosmoGIRL!* and regular *Cosmo*. You'd think she was operating a newsstand out of there.

Choosing my "Vintage Vanguard Vixens" iPod playlist (Liz Phair, Ani DiFranco, Sarah McLachlan, Alanis Morissette), I could feel the singers' disdain oozing out the speakers as I flipped through the pages of anorexic supermodels with perfect skin. "Yeah, well, maybe if I had a guitar and an ounce of musical talent, I wouldn't have to stoop to this," I said to the speakers. The magazines may have been able to tell you Ten Ways to Make Him Yours (*Find out what perfume his mother wears and then buy some for yourself! Chant his name 108 times before you go to bed for thirty-three days!*), but they sure didn't bother telling you Ten Ways to Put on Mascara Without Ending Up with a Detached Retina.

This seemed to be a learn-by-doing situation, so I hauled the cosmetic care package into my bathroom to get to work. Unlike the Clones' bathrooms, mine was very neat. Shampoo and conditioner bottles lined up by size, towels perfectly folded . . . okay, maybe I was a *little* OCD. I took the cover off the container and stared at the jumble of little tubes and compacts and pencils, took a deep breath, crossed myself like Catholics always did in movies (even though I'm Jewish, I figured it couldn't hurt), and went to work.

After a half hour of brushing and curling and dotting and blending, I stood back from the mirror to take a look at myself. It was hard to see because I had poked myself in the eye repeatedly while trying to put on eyeliner, but from what I could make out, I don't think I had "enhanced" anything. Instead I looked like a drag queen who had been made up by a blind person.

My blue eye shadow had somehow made its way over to my temples, and there were all these little dots from the mascara under my eyebrows. Or what *used* to be my eyebrows before I made the mistake of tweezing them. The eyeliner had given me a raccoon effect and the blush looked like two big angry red gashes. And to top it off, there was more lipstick on my teeth than on my lips.

"Omigod," I said to the mirror. I was a bona fide hootchie. At least from the neck up.

I went into my bedroom, hoping that somehow my reflection would look less frightening there. Apparently not. As Alanis warbled away about how ironic life was, my face began to itch, so I went into Clarissa's bathroom to get some cold cream to take it all off. Which, I soon discovered, was almost as difficult as putting it on. By the time I was done scrubbing my face, it was almost ready to blister.

Like BklynBoy said, I was going to have to be myself when it came to Noah—or at least look like myself.

Because I sure wasn't doing *this* again.

chapter eight

Sunday may have been the Lord's day for the rest of the world, but it was my day to work at Blissed Out. Technically, I wasn't supposed to work there because I'm only fifteen, but India's parents were so thrilled that I wanted to "give back to the community" that they hired me and paid me under the table. All I had to do was say *"Namaste"* to people when they walked in and make sure they signed in and ring up whatever overpriced clothing they got in the boutique. Boring, yes, but a lot better than working in the food industry, where I would have had to wear a polyester smock and a hairnet. And I got to take all the free yoga classes that I wanted. *If* I had wanted to. I tried one class, but I couldn't stop laughing and the teacher asked me to leave.

Around 2 P.M. I was behind the sign-in desk with Phoolendu. Up until three years earlier, Phoolendu had been known as Joshua Craig Samuels of Encino, California, and spent most of his free time surfing out at Point Dume in Malibu. From some pictures he had shown me, he had been pretty cute, if you went for the surfer-dude type. After graduating from UC Santa Barbara, he went to Bali to surf and ended up in India, where he realized that, in actuality, his existence as Josh was just an illusion and that his true self was this guy named Phoolendu, which means "Full Moon" in Hindu. He even went as far as to have it legally changed. After that he wasn't so cute. Well, he was if you liked guys who had dreadlocks down the middle of their backs and didn't believe in deodorant.

In the beginning, working with Phoo was pretty uncomfortable—not only because of the lack of deodorant, but because he wasn't a big talker, which made me feel compelled to nervously fill every minute of airspace with chatter. He said I shouldn't take it personally—that most of the time he was meditating, even if it didn't look like it because his eyes were open, but I think it was because he used to smoke a ton of pot before getting into yoga, so he didn't have many brain cells left. At any rate, I had gotten used to it (the fact that his new girlfriend had turned him on to an organic, no-animals-harmed deodorant helped) and now, when he did talk, it was exciting. Like listening to the Dalai Lama. Had we met in the real world instead of at work, we probably wouldn't have been friends, but I had really come to love him. That is, when I could understand what he was talking about.

We had just recovered from the sign-in rush for the two o'clock class and I had gone back to Googling Noah on the Internet (a few short stories on various webzines that I'd print out later and read) as I waited for it to be two-thirty so I could go meet India and Malcolm at Café du Village for lunch. Then it hit me—why not ask someone who spent all his time trying to become enlightened about my love life? I figured whatever he'd say would be just as good if not better than what Dr. Greenburg would have to say on Tuesday.

"Hey, Phoo?" I said, making sure to close out of the Internet window in case our manager, Parvati, walked by.

"Yes, Cindy?" he said softly as he looked up from his *Hindu Gods and Goddesses for Dummies* book. At least that's what I thought he said. In addition to not being a big talker, Phoo was also a low talker.

"Can I ask you a question?" I asked. I could hear the class in the small room begin the chanting portion of the practice.

"Of course you can, Cindy. However, that's rather redundant because isn't life itself just one big question?" he asked as he gathered his hair into a ponytail. Phoo was always throwing out heavy stuff like that. Sometimes it was so deep that I was left with a headache.

"Um, I guess so. Anyway, so I have this dilemma—" I said.

He chuckled. If you've ever seen the Dalai Lama on the

news, he chuckles, too. "Oh, Cindy, isn't *life* just one big dilemma?" he said.

"Sure, but this one is kind of . . . time sensitive."

Another chuckle. "Cindy, wouldn't you say that time—"

This conversation was going to take forever. "Phoo, can I be the one asking the questions today?"

He nodded.

"Thank you. So my question today has to do with fate versus free will," I said. The chanting began to get louder. It was like listening to a gospel choir, but in Hindu.

He nodded gravely. "Ah, yes. The age-old question. In fact, I was meditating on that just this morning."

"Great. Then you'll definitely be able to help me. See, I have a hunch that I may have met my soul mate yesterday—"

"But I thought Adam Silver was your soul mate?"

"Yeah, but this guy is my *soul-mate* soul mate."

"Well, If he's truly your soul-mate soul mate, Cindy, then it wouldn't be a hunch. It might start off as a hunch, but it would quickly blossom into a deep, inner knowing that you'd feel in your root chakra," he explained.

"Wait, where's the root chakra again?"

Phoo pointed to the area at the base of my spine, which, I had learned in my one and only yoga class, was called the sacrum. I tried to remember if anything had been going on there yesterday, but those chairs at Starbucks were superuncomfortable, so it was hard to say.

"I'm not sure. But here's my question: if this guy truly is my soul mate, then he'd love me just the way I am, right? I mean, I wouldn't have to wear a lot of makeup, or act like a stupid girl who doesn't know how to open a door for herself, or dress like Paris Hilton . . . "

"Paris who?"

"Never mind. What I'm saying is that if it's fate, then we'll just end up together, right?"

"Well, the short answer is yes. However, it might not happen in this particular lifetime. You see, you both may need to go through the cycle of *samskara shuddhi* many times before you actually 'hook up,' as you Westerners like to say," he said.

"I hate to have to keep telling you this, Phoo, but you're a Westerner, too, even if you did change your name," I replied. "So sam what?"

"*Samskara shuddhi.* It's the cleansing of past traumas and negative behavior patterns."

"Interesting. But I don't think this guy has a lot of negative behavior patterns. At least none that I picked up on. And, as for me, I've already been in therapy for almost four years, so do you think that maybe that means we might end up together sooner?" I asked hopefully.

Phoo stroked his soul patch. "That's an interesting question. I'll meditate on that tonight and e-mail you in the morning."

I went back to checking out Noah online when I heard

footsteps coming up the stairs. There was this saying I once heard on *Oprah*: "You make your plans and God laughs." Well, my plan had been never to see Adam Silver again after bombarding him with maxi pads, so you can imagine how confused I was when I looked up to see . . . *Adam Silver*. In my place of work. On a day when I had no eyebrows and a red face because of the makeup incident.

"Omigod!" I croaked before ducking underneath the counter.

"What is it?" said Phoo.

"It's Adam Silver!" I hissed.

"Talk about *kismet*!" he hissed back.

"I can't let him see me—I don't have any eyebrows!" I whispered.

I could hear Adam's Pumas on the hardwood floors. What was going on here? For almost two years I hadn't been able to get within a five-mile radius of the guy and now, when I was at my lowest, he was everywhere.

"*Namaste*," I heard Phoo say. "Welcome to Blissed Out."

"Um, hey," I heard Adam reply. "My sisters and I want to get my mom some yoga classes for her birthday. Do you have a gift certificate or something like that?"

"Sure," said Phoo. "Let me find them . . . they're here somewhere." As he rooted through the messy pile of flyers (chakra balancing workshops and raw food extravaganzas) and business cards (colonics and dog psychics) on the counter, his Birkenstocks started kicking up the dust bunnies underneath. When my nose began to tickle, I could tell a sneeze wasn't far off.

"So has your mother visited us before or is she new to the ancient practice of yoga?" Phoo asked.

The sneeze was getting closer.

The sound of clapping now joined the chanting from the other room. "She's, uh, new," Adam said, sounding freaked out. "Her Pilates teacher decided she's only focusing on celebrity clients from now on, so she's looking to do something new." There was a hole underneath the counter, so I was able to watch him while Phoo looked for the gift certificates. Well, I was able to look at his jeans and sneakers. As I got closer to the wood to try to get a better look, the sneeze bloomed and I hit my head. "Ow," I whispered.

"God bless you," Phoo said.

"Huh?" Adam said.

"I was just . . . blessing you," said Phoo. "We like to bless all our customers." I shook my head underneath the counter. Phoo was hopeless when it came to lying. "By the way, I'm Phoolendu."

"Adam," I heard him say before I sneezed again. And again. "Is there . . . someone down there?" he asked suspiciously.

I couldn't bear listening to Phoo come up with another bad lie, so I took a deep breath and stood up nonchalantly like there was nothing strange about the fact that I had been hanging out on a dirty, dusty floor behind the counter of a yoga studio. In fact, I was so nonchalant that at first I just ignored Adam and started shuffling papers around on the counter. Then, calling on the one acting class I had taken at camp when I was twelve, I looked up and tried to appear what I hoped resembled something along the lines of "startled, but able to remain calm."

"Oh. Hello," I said in my startled-but-calm voice.

"Hey," he said, surprised to see me. "Don't tell me you wiped out again," he teased.

"No. I was just . . . looking for this," I said, bending down and picking up the first thing my hand landed on, which happened to be an XL women's sports bra from the lost-and-found carton.

I don't know who turned more red when I held it up—him or me.

"So, uh, you work here?" he asked.

I cleared my throat. "Well, on Sundays I do." I tried to think of something else to say. "The other days I go to school. Not on Saturdays, but during the week . . . " *Pleaseshutup, pleaseshutup,* I said to myself.

As Phoo continued to make more of a mess, I tried not to stare at how Adam's Bob Dylan T-shirt hugged his tan arms in just the right places. Another Dylan fan—just like BklynBoy. I wondered if Noah liked him, too.

Thuds now joined the clapping and the chanting, along with an occasional wail.

"What are they *doing* in there?" asked Adam.

I dared myself to look up. "Sometimes, if they get really blissed out from the chanting, some of them get up and start jumping around the room," I explained before looking back down again.

"You should come check it out one day!" said Phoo. "It's amazing. Think of your best acid trip ever and multiply it by a hundred."

"Uh, yeah, maybe," said Adam, which had a "not on your life" undertone to it.

We were all quiet again.

"That's a cool T-shirt," he said a moment later.

"Thanks," I said, my heart rate revving up even higher. I was wearing my ANXIETY BURNS A LOT OF CALORIES one, which, at that moment, couldn't have been a truer statement. My mouth opened like I was going to say something else, but I couldn't think of anything, so I closed it again. Great—I was turning into a guppy.

"So do you do yoga?" Adam asked.

I couldn't believe he was continuing to attempt to have a conversation with me when it was painfully obvious that I was socially handicapped.

"Me?"

"Yeah."

Another lort. "Um, no."

"Being with her breath is still somewhat frightening to Cindy," Phoo piped up. "How about you, Adam? Have you allowed yourself to enjoy the many benefits that yoga has to offer?" He sounded like a bad infomercial.

"Actually . . ." Adam began to say.

". . . he plays soccer," I said. "And basketball. And baseball. He doesn't have time for yoga." So much for not coming off as a stalker. It got quiet again and I went back to looking at the desk.

"Hey, you ran off the other day before I had a chance to tell you I really liked that piece you wrote for the paper about how stupid the prom is," he said.

I looked up. "How'd you know I wrote it?" I asked warily.

"Um, let's see . . . because you're Cindy Gold?"

"But how do you know my name?" I asked. Now I was just plain mystified.

Phoo's head was going back and forth like he was watching a tennis match.

Adam's laugh was almost as great as Noah's. "It's not *that* big of a school. Anyway, I thought it was really well written."

"You did?" I said, turning even more red.

"Yeah. Dude, it took a lot of guts to say some of that stuff!"

Dude. My heart sank. I was just another dude in Adam Silver's eyes.

"You didn't tell me you wrote a piece for the paper," said Phoo. "How wonderful! I think it's fantastic that you're channeling your disillusionment with Western society in such a healthy way. You know, the written word has the power to affect so many people—"

"Thanks," I mumbled. "Why don't you try to find a gift certificate for . . . it's Adam, right?" I was trying to "act like you care less" like I'd read in *CosmoGIRL!* the night before, but it didn't feel so good.

"Yeah," he replied, eyeing me strangely. Since I knew his afterschool sports schedule, I guess he figured I'd know his name.

The door to the small room opened and out filed fifteen dazed-looking students, covered with sweat. The heavy smell of patchouli and Fleur de Thé perfume hit my nostrils as they padded past the desk and we all sneezed in unison.

"Here they are!" exclaimed Phoo. "They were on top of the pile the whole time!" He chuckled. "So what denomination would you like the gift certificate, Adam?"

"A hundred, please," Adam said, taking out a wad of crumpled bills.

As Phoo and I watched him count them out, I could feel myself wanting to chew on the ends of my hair, another one of my nervous habits, and had to grip the counter to keep myself from doing it. I'm sure I looked like an actress in one of those re-creations of an earthquake on some low-budget docudrama, but I didn't want to take any chances of embarrassing myself any more than I already had.

"Well, it was cool running into you," Adam said after

he was done paying, and held out his hand to shake mine.

Except that I couldn't shake his because I was still gripping the counter and my hands were clammy with sweat. "Uh, yeah. I guess I'll see you around school sometime," I mumbled, staring at one of the moving dust bunnies on the floor.

"Okay. Bye." He looked over at Phoo. "Take it easy, dude." I perked up—maybe everyone was a dude in Adam's eyes, male or female. It was nice to know he didn't discriminate.

"Oh, I always do. *Namaste*, Adam," Phoo replied.

After I heard the door close behind him, I exhaled all the breath that I had been holding. "That was beyond embarrassing," I moaned. "Now I'm definitely going to have to transfer to finish out the year."

Phoo chuckled. "Don't worry, Cindy. Thankfully the only person you embarrassed yourself in front of was me, and you know how nonjudgmental I am," he said, patting my arm.

I grabbed my bag from underneath the counter. "I'm going to lunch now so I can stuff my shame down with some fries," I said. "Want anything?"

"An Acai Supercharger with a Fiber Boost from Jamba Juice would be great."

Forget the beauty makeover—I need a personality makeover, I thought as I walked down Larchmont to Café du Village. By the time I got there, India and Malcolm were already sitting at an outside table talking to Gilles, one of the waiters, in French. Well, India was *trying* to speak French, but from the look of confusion on Gilles's face, she wasn't doing a very good job. Not that it mattered—he would have sat there and listened to her speak Pig Latin for the next five hours. Gilles had a massive crush on her. *Everyone* at Café du Village did, including Chou Chou, the owner's pug, who wouldn't stop humping her leg. To everyone else (i.e., me) they were just their normal French selves (i.e., rude) but I didn't make a big deal about it because they always brought us a crème brûlée on the house in their attempts to impress India. Ironic, considering that India couldn't even have one bite, since she doesn't eat sugar.

"You're so not going to believe what just happened," I squealed as I sat down. "Hey, Gilles," I said. "Can I get a Coke and a turkey burger, please? And some extra fries? Thanks."

"*Excusez-moi?*" he said.

"Une Coke, une turkey burger, et très beaucoup fries," I said slowly. "Merci."

He cringed at my butchering of the French language and muttered something under his breath as he went to get my food and I tried to slow my racing heart. All the drama made me feel like I was going to pass out.

"What's that rash on your face?" Malcolm asked.

"Allergic reaction to the makeup. So I'm standing there with Phoo—"

"What happened to your eyebrows?" he demanded.

"Nothing. So I'm standing there with Phoo—"

"What do you mean 'nothing'? No one tweezes their eyebrows that much except girlfriends of gang members," he said.

"I was *experimenting*, Malcolm, as part of *Operation Turn Cindy into a Girl,* and obviously things got a little out of hand. So we're standing—"

"You weren't supposed to do anything *unsupervised*," he replied. "Why didn't you wait—"

"Malcolm," I sighed. "Remember a few weeks ago we had that little talk about interrupting?"

"Right. I'm sorry. Go on," he said.

"Thank you. So, like I was saying, I'm standing there with Phoo—"

"How is he, by the way?" asked Malcolm.

"He's fine. So I'm standing—"

"My mom said she ran into him and his girlfriend at the colonics place the other day and she's like supermodel hot," said India.

"Um, guys? I'm in severe crisis mode at the moment," I said.

"Oooh! You didn't mention it was a *crisis*!" Malcolm said gleefully. "So what happened?!"

"So Adam Silver came into the studio to buy his mother a gift certificate," I blurted out before I could be interrupted again.

"Omigod. That's twice in one week!" said India.

"I know. And ready for this? He knew my name."

An audible gasp rose up.

"And not only that, but he read The Letter and thought it was quote-really-well-written-end-quote."

"Oh. My. God," said Malcolm.

"I know," I said.

"So then what happened," asked India.

"Um, let's see . . . well, then I acted like a total idiot, and couldn't even shake his hand good-bye because mine were so clammy."

"Omigod," said India.

"I know," I said.

"You're lucky there's only a few more weeks of school left and he's a senior," said Malcolm.

"I know. Which is why pulling off *Operation Turn Cindy into a Girl* is so important, you guys, so that this kind of tragedy isn't repeated on Thursday when I see Noah."

Gilles put my turkey burger down in front of me, and I started shoving fries in my mouth. Apparently, much like love, humiliation makes you hungry. As Malcolm rambled on about how we could intensify our efforts to make it safe for me to be around boys without supervision, I looked up from my food and nearly choked. *Noah* was walking down Larchmont toward us—with an ETA of oh, about, *thirty* seconds. Definitely not enough time to complete *Operation Turn Cindy into a Girl.*

"I cannot believe this," I whispered after I was done coughing.

"What?" said Malcolm indignantly. "You *said* you'd be willing to go to any length to win Noah's heart."

For the second time that day, I got down on my knees and tried to hide from a cute boy. This time I squatted under the table as if I was looking for my fork.

But I wasn't quick enough.

"Cindy?" said Noah, sizzling in his Adidas track pants and a vintage Nirvana T-shirt. "Is that you?"

I climbed out from under the table. "Noah! Hi!" I said. "Malcolm and India, this is my new SAT tutor, Noah."

Noah looked at me for a minute. "You look . . . different," he said. "Did you cut your hair?"

"It's her eyebrows," said India.

"Oh. Well, they look . . . nice. So I guess you're the mayor of Larchmont Boulevard."

"Huh?"

"You know, since I just saw you over there less than twenty-four hours ago—" He pointed to our Starbucks across the street.

"Oh, right!" I said, and started fake laughing. *Ground, please open and swallow me up NOW*, I thought to myself.

Noah gave me a weird look. "So are you eating here?" I asked. *Pleasesayno, pleasesayno*, I prayed.

"No." There was a God. "I'm on my way to my book-club meeting over on Lucerne."

Malcolm's eyebrows shot up. "You're in a book club?"

"Yeah."

"What book are you guys reading?" he asked.

"*Edie* by George Plimpton. Have you heard of it?" Noah asked.

Again with the eyebrows. "Oh, *sure*," said Malcolm. "Who *doesn't* know who Edie Sedgwick is?"

"I don't," piped up India. "Who is she?"

"The girl that the movie *Factory Girl* was based on," Malcolm replied.

"Oh. Did anyone even see that? It came and went so quickly," India said, as if this was a cocktail party on a yacht instead of one of the most embarrassing moments of my life.

Noah looked at his watch. "I should get going, I'm already pretty late." He turned to me. "So I'll see you here on Thursday?"

I nodded. I couldn't wait for him to leave. A girl could take only so much humiliation in one day.

He flashed a smile at India and Malcolm. "Nice meeting you."

"You, too," they said in unison.

As he left I reached for Malcolm's fries. The only way to deal with this was to eat as many carbs as I could get my hands on.

"Oh, Cin," said Malcolm. "I am *so* sorry to have to be the one to tell you this,"

"What? That I'm so completely hopeless that you don't even think *Operation Turn Cindy into a Girl* is even worth it anymore?" I asked glumly.

"No. To tell you that . . ." He looked around to make sure no one was listening and lowered his voice. ". . . Noah's . . ." He looked around one more time to be safe. ". . . *gay*," he said loudly.

I closed my eyes and focused on the point in between my now almost nonexistent eyebrows that Phoo told me was called my third eye so I could center myself and calm down.

I opened my eyes. "Malcolm, you think *every* cute boy is gay or at least seriously confused!" I shrieked.

I could tell by the way his eyes were narrowing that he was about to start channeling his inner diva. He started huffing and puffing, tsking, and if he had had long hair, he definitely would've flipped it.

"Cindy. Ella. Gold. I cannot believe you're questioning me on this. What's the one other thing I'm an expert on other than Madonna lyrics?" he demanded.

"Eighties teen movies?" suggested India.

"Other than that," said Malcolm.

I crossed my arms in front of my chest and refused to look at him. I knew where he was going with this.

"Cindy, answer me," he demanded.

"I don't know." I pouted.

"Oh, yes you do," he said, and moved his chair so that

he was in my line of sight. I moved *my* chair so that my back was to him.

Malcolm sighed so loud that I'm sure BklynBoy heard him all the way in New York. *"Gaydar,"* he said.

"Well, obviously it's not working today," I said stubbornly.

"I'm telling you—he's gay," Malcolm said.

"How would you know that? You spent like a minute and a half in his presence and I've spent, like . . . *ninety*!"

"Cindy, he's in a *book club.*"

"So?! He's a writer! If he's a writer, that means he's a reader!" I cried.

"Yeah, but don't you know that Edie Sedgwick is like one of *the* patron saints of hip gay men of his generation?" he asked.

"I have to tell you, I'm still not all that clear on who Edie Sedgwick is," India said. "Is she related to Kyra?"

"Maybe it just means he's a drug addict," I retorted.

"Can someone please fill me in here?" India whined.

Malcolm turned to her. "She was this rich society girl who started hanging out with Andy Warhol in the sixties and wore black tights and had silver hair and got really into speed and OD'd."

India wrinkled her nose. "Ew. And they made a movie about her? Why?"

"Because she was totally fabulous, India." He sighed. "Obviously you had to be there."

He turned to me. "And it's not just the book club that makes me think he's gay. It's also my intuition. Remember, that psychic Sola told me that I'm *very* intuitive."

"What do you mean 'you had to be there'? *You* weren't there," said India, who wasn't good at letting things go.

"So what! Sola told me the exact same thing!" I shot back. But it was getting more and more difficult to keep up my front. Malcolm wasn't kidding about his gaydar skills. I'm not going to list them here because I don't want to get sued or anything, but I can't *tell* you how many people— including some very well-known actors—he's been right about. However, I wasn't ready to give in just yet. "Fine. I'll find out for sure on Thursday when I see him," I said. "But I'm telling you—you're wrong about this one."

"And let me guess who decided you'd meet here," Malcolm said smugly, like a gay Encyclopedia Brown.

"What? It's quiet," I said. "Plus, it's the only place on the street that's not overrun by Marlborough girls with their uniform skirts rolled up to their crotches." Marlborough was a private girls' school down the street.

Malcolm rolled his eyes. "Seems to me he likes the French. That's all I'm saying." He didn't *have* to say more.

"You're going to straight out ask him if he's gay?" said India.

"Of course not. I'll just . . . Don't you worry how I do it. The important part is that I will," I replied. I looked around for Gilles. "Where's Gilles? He better bring us a crème brûlée today."

India shut her eyes tight. "Um, I was going to wait and do this tomorrow, but as long as we're on the subject of bad news, there's something I need to tell you," she said.

"What?" I sighed.

"Jacksonaskedmetothepromandl'mgoing," she said with her eyes still shut. Jackson Connolly was a senior with whom India had bonded one day in the school parking lot when she saw the "Be Kind to Animals—Don't Eat Them" bumper sticker on his Volvo. She liked to say they had dated for two months before he broke up with her to go out with Maya Mornell, but the truth is it was mostly an e-lationship that took place through e-mail and texts.

"Wait a second—you had a Jamba Juice with the guy once and you're going to commit to spending *five whole hours* with him?" I asked.

She shrugged. "I feel bad for him. He was supposed to go with Maya, but she called him last night to say she'd rather go to the Palisades prom with Russell Robinson."

"Jeez, is *every* high school in Los Angeles having their prom on the same night?" I asked.

"Pretty much," replied Malcolm.

"Look, it's not like I'm excited about it or anything," said India. "It's just a mercy date."

When Gilles set the crème brûlée down on the table, I attacked it. *What* was going on? First, I embarrassed myself in front of the most popular guy in school, then I learned that my soul mate/future husband/father of my children might be gay, and now I was being told that I was about to be the only Los Angeles resident over the age of ten who wouldn't be attending one of the thousand proms that would be taking place across the city in approximately nine days and five hours because both my best friends had gone over to the other side, leaving me to be my own little island.

As Gilles walked by again, I grabbed his arm. "Gilles, hit me again," I said, pointing to the empty crème brûlée dish.

With the kind of day I was having, it was going to take an all-day *Sex and the City* marathon, a Molly Ringwald retrospective, *and* a gallon of Chunky Monkey to make me feel better.

chapter nine

Dr. Greenburg always says that dreams are an X-ray of what's going on in the psyche. Or, in the case of my recurring one—the one where I get the longest standing ovation in the history of *The Oprah Winfrey* show when I go on to talk about my best-selling, critically acclaimed debut novel—wish fulfillment. Anyway, my dream on Sunday night had been so intense that I woke up that Monday (twenty minutes late, because of a short power outage, as evidenced by the blinking numbers on my digital clock) unable to shake it.

In the dream, instead of following me out to the lunch tree, India and Malcolm had gone and sat down at Madison Smallwood's table—Madison, as the most popular girl in the sophomore class, had been asked to the prom back in October—and proceeded to crack up after Malcolm gave me his patented up-down-up-again raise-of-the-eyebrows stare and started whispering.

I just knew that the prom would be the thing that ended our friendship. Not India and Malcolm's friendship, but *my* friendship with them because they'd be spending all their time together shopping for dresses and tuxes, and getting manicures, and doing hair and makeup run-throughs. All stuff that there'd be no reason for me to do with them, not only because I wasn't going, but because—as evidenced by Saturday night's L.A. Tweezer Massacre—playing Barbie Beauty Salon wasn't my thing to begin with.

Before I knew it, my only friend would be Spencer, which was beyond pathetic and didn't count because he was a year old and couldn't talk. I might as well just get my GED through the mail. Forget about going to NYU and ending up a famous novelist—I'd be lucky if I was made head barista at Starbucks one day.

Maybe I was engaging in catastrophic thinking, which, according to Dr. Greenburg, I was prone to because of my mother's untimely death, but the dream, along with the MMBs (Monday Morning Blahs) and the power outage that had me doing the brushing teeth/yanking on jeans/ swiping deodorant multitasking dance, didn't put me in the best mood that morning.

There was nothing more depressing than a Monday morning, except maybe that last hour of Sunday night TV that you can't enjoy because you're already obsessing about the fact that once you go to bed, you're going to wake up to Monday morning. Not only were there five days until the weekend, but soon I'd have to find a new tree in the farthest corner of campus that provided enough shade so that I wouldn't end up at the dermatologist's office having melanoma patches removed every other day when I was fifty.

Apparently the power outage had been citywide because India was fifteen minutes late to pick me up. "Don't slam it so hard! You'll break it!"she snapped as I got into Goldie Hawn.

"Sorry," I snapped back, mad at her for replacing me with Madison Smallwood. "I just don't feel like falling out of the car on the way to school."

Before I could even put my seat belt on, India was tearing down our driveway like it was the last lap of the Indy 500.

"India. Just breathe," I ordered as I kissed my finger and tapped the ceiling as we barreled through a just-turned-red light on Beverly Boulevard. India driving while calm was a nerve-wracking experience, but getting in the car with her when she was upset was a death wish. "I bet you everyone's going to be late," I offered. "And if worse comes to worst, we'll get you a letter from the electric company so nothing goes on your record."

She relaxed a little and stopped tailgating the carpool-driving mom in the BMW SUV in front of us who kept giving us the finger. "You think they'd do that?"

"Sure," I replied. "Especially if you told them that an

award for Perfect Attendance would put you over the top with the Stanford admission committee. Public utility companies are a sucker for that kind of stuff," I said.

"You're probably right," she agreed, back to her mellow self that I knew and loved.

I knew I was about to push my luck, but I decided to give it a try. "Hey, can we stop at Urth Caffe? Ashley fell off the green-foods wagon last night and went on a major binge, so now there's nothing in the house other than some stale Triscuits."

"And be even later? No way!" she replied as she cut off a bus. "Check in my bag. I think I have some sunflower seeds."

I rolled my eyes. "I'll just wait till we get to school. I've got a box of Hot Tamales in my locker."

She rolled her eyes back. "I'm telling you—sometimes I have no idea how we're friends."

There it was. My paranoia *wasn't* just paranoia. I knew Sola had been right when she said I was an incredibly intuitive person.

As we began the slow crawl up Coldwater Canyon, India turned to me and put her hand on my shoulder. "Cin, there's something I want to talk to you about—"

I sucked in my breath. I hadn't known I was going to be dumped before we even got to school.

"Okay, now I want you to be completely honest with me—are you *sure* you're okay with me going to the prom with Jackson? Because if you're not, I won't go."

I opened my mouth to tell her that, actually, if she wanted to know the truth, I *was* bummed because I was afraid it would mean I'd lose her as a friend. In addition to vulnerability, the other issue that Dr. Greenburg and I were working on was my fear of confrontation, and this was the perfect opportunity to work on that, had I been able to get a word in.

"You see, I was thinking about it all night and the truth is that I never could have gone out on a limb like you did with your letter and I'm just so blown away by your courage. And it's really important to me that I support your empowerment—not only as a fellow woman, but as your best friend in the entire universe. So if you just want to order in from Real Food Daily that night and watch *Valley Girl* together, I'm totally into that."

I may not have been able to apply eye shadow correctly, but I did know how to pick my friends. I was so moved by her loyalty that I wanted to cry.

"Okay, (A) I can't tell you how much it means to me that you would do that, but (B) as strong as my feelings might be about this whole issue, I think you should go. Jackson's a really sweet guy and you'll be doing him a huge favor," I said. "Oh, and (C), if there has to be a prom, there should at least be some cool people like you and Malcolm there to balance out all the negative energy of the Clones and company. There's just one thing I need you to promise me."

"What?"

"That you won't dump me for Madison Smallwood."

India scrunched up her nose like a bunny and narrowed her eyes. "What are you talking about?"

I shrugged. "I just got worried that you'd end up sitting with her at the prom and that would lead to you guys moving into the cafeteria to eat lunch with her, and before I knew it, you'd pull a Staci Woodman on me." Staci Woodman was this girl whose two best friends, Lucy and Ondine, called her up the morning of her bat mitzvah and told her they wouldn't be coming because they no longer wanted to be friends with her.

"Okay, first of all, Lucy and Ondine were *totally* right to do that because Staci Woodman is a kleptomaniac psycho—don't you remember I told you she stole like five of my Beanie Babies that time I let her sleep over my house in second grade?—and second of all, I can't believe that after all these years you wouldn't know that nothing like that would ever happen because we're going to be best friends forever and have a double wedding and have our babies at the same time."

After that, I *did* start crying. "Thanks," I said as I dabbed at my eyes with a crumpled-up napkin I found on the floor. "I guess with it being Monday and all, I just feel kind of vulnerable."

India reached over and hugged me. "Wow. My parents would be so impressed if I could label my feelings like that.

Hey, I know you're going to be a famous writer, but you should also think about getting your Ph.D. and becoming a shrink, too. You're awesome with this stuff."

Our BFF bonding moment was broken by angry honks, seeing that we had missed the light turning green. India popped her head out the window. "Jesus Christ, it's Monday morning—what the hell are you people in a hurry for?! It's not going to make the day go by any faster!" she screamed. I guess you could meditate and *Om* all you wanted, but the frustration of living in a major metropolis had to go somewhere. I was just waiting for the day when the news had a story about a yogi who went postal in McDonald's.

We were a half hour late by the time we got to school, but from the amount of kids in the parking lot, so was everyone else. Including Malcolm.

"Wow. Something huge must have happened for him to be out here," I said as we chugged into a parking space. Malcolm was standing apart from the clusters of smokers, frantically waving his hands in front of his face, as if that was going to put a dent in the cloud of cigarette smoke that had taken up permanent residence there since 1982.

As soon as he saw—or rather heard—us, he marched over, tapping his foot impatiently as I went through the daily routine of jiggling the door handle to get myself out of the death trap while praying it didn't break off. By the time I succeeded, the tapping turned to hopping.

"Jeez, Malcolm. You better calm down before you have an asthma attack," I said as I climbed out and hitched up my jeans. I so hoped they'd someday start making jeans again that actually covered your entire butt. "What's going on?"

"You're not going to believe this—" he said, pausing to have a melodramatic coughing fit as Paige Darnell walked by and exhaled. Paige had adopted Courtney Love as her role model (complete with rehab stints, baby-doll dresses, and torn black stockings) and I always felt like I needed a shower after being around her.

"What?! What?!" asked India, jumping up and down in tree pose.

He took a deep breath. "Okay, so Jessica Rokosny?"

India and I took in our own deep breaths and nodded in unison.

"Not only did she get drunk and end up hooking up with Asher again—" he said (Asher was Jessica's boyfriend until he walked in on her and his twenty-two-year-old cousin who was visiting from France), "but *then* they hooked up with Hilary Tilton!" Hilary had been Asher's girlfriend before she walked in on him and Jessica in Adam Silver's bathroom during a party.

India turned to me. "Omigod—you're so in the clear. That totally trumps The Letter as good gossip!"

I could feel the stress of the last week draining out of my toes. Maybe there *was* a God.

"Wait—it gets better," said Malcolm. "But then the whole thing ended with a *catfight* between Jessica and Hilary! God, I wish I had been there to see it." He sighed. "It sounds so Aaron Spelling." He opened his arms. "Group hug?"

India and I fell into them and the three of us jumped up and down and squealed. When we broke apart, Adam Silver was directly in my line of vision. Smiling at me. At least it *looked* like a smile, but because my sunglasses had gotten knocked off mid-hug and the sun was now blinding me, it was hard to tell.

"Oh. Um. Hi. We were just . . . " I trailed off. Just what? Taking pleasure in someone else's misfortune? Yeah, that would make me out to be a nice person.

"Really excited about the fact that it's Monday and we have another five days until the weekend?" Adam guessed. The smile—or whatever it was—was still there.

"Um . . . yeah . . . something like that," I replied, before crouching down to pick up my glasses, therefore giving him a full-on view of my butt crack.

"Well, I hope it's a good one," he said as he ambled off.

Jessica Rokosny was immediately forgotten. Malcolm turned to me. "You know, I don't want to give you any sort of false hope, seeing that he's the most popular guy in school and you're considered crazy by everyone other than me and India, but I just have to say that the way he was looking at you was *exactly* the way Blane looks at

Andie when he comes into the record store in *Pretty in Pink*."

"Really?" asked India. "I sort of thought it was more like how Randy looks at Julie at the club when they first meet in *Valley Girl*. You know, that 'we're totally soul mates' look?"

As the bell rang and we made our way to the building (they walked, I floated), the two of them continued to bicker over what Adam's eyes and body language were saying during the five-second exchange between us while I tried to figure out how it was possible that no matter how many times I embarrassed myself in front of Adam Silver, he still continued to talk to me.

But once inside the building, I fell from cloud nine to the depths of hell. The usually bare walls were covered with Photoshopped campaign posters for Prom Queen and King wannabes while their real-life counterparts handed out buttons (*You can't go wrong with Suzy Long as Prom Queen!*), monogrammed pens and pencils (*Dude, write this down: Matt Kring for Prom King*), and—in Dylan Schoenfield's case—swag bags filled with makeup, gift certificates, and American Apparel tank tops (*Dylan Schoenfield for Prom Queen—that's so hot*).

"This has got to be illegal," I said.

"How so?" yelled Malcolm over his shoulder as he tried to push his way through the massive crowd gathered near Dylan's camp and grab a gift bag.

"This is a school—not a boutique on Robertson!" I said.

"But they're not selling anything. They're giving it away, so I think that protects them from breaking the 'no soliciting' rule," replied India.

"They are too selling something," I retorted, frustrated that no one but me saw the insanity of the situation. "They're selling their *souls*."

Mission accomplished, Malcolm rejoined us. "Um, excuse me, but *I'm* the drama queen angel in this friendship, thankyouverymuch. Not to mention it so doesn't suit you." Suddenly he stopped walking. "Oh. No," he whispered.

"What?" I said, over my shoulder. "Is the tank top not your size?"

When he didn't respond, I turned toward where he was looking.

For once, Malcolm was being understated. It was more like "OHMYGODOHMYGODOHMYGOD." Because at the end of the hall, right near the cafeteria, was my pre-Clarissa eighth-grade yearbook photo—complete with a Supercuts haircut and the world's most hideous glasses—blown up to poster size. I looked like a female Harry Potter in his gawkiest stage. Underneath the picture it said *Don't be like SOME people and miss out on what's sure to be one of the most important events of your entire life. And don't miss out on voting for Dakota Greene for Prom Queen!*

For once I was in full agreement with the Clones on something: Dakota Greene *was* the biggest hoochie hoodrat at Castle Heights. She was also the *meanest* hoochie hoodrat in the entire world.

India's sonic-boom-level gasp didn't help the situation. It only made a group of juniors walking by glance over at us, then at the poster, then at us again, before cracking up.

I had seen the movie *Election*—I knew how certain girls would stop at nothing to get what they wanted. But this was beyond disgusting.

"This is beyond disgusting," I announced.

"Yeah, with all that money she has, you'd think she'd just *buy* her votes," Malcolm added.

A spidery pair of arms grabbed my shoulders from behind. "Oh. My. God. Cindy! Are you just *totally* freaking out right now?" squealed Ashley. "Because that is like *the* meanest thing I've ever seen!"

Britney joined her and patted me on the arm. "I totally forgot how bad that picture was. You know, you could probably sue her if you wanted to," she offered.

Ashley was right—this *did* win first price for evilness. Maybe our blended family just needed an extreme crisis like this to bring us together. Maybe now we'd have a chance to bond like *real* sisters.

I smiled. "Well, I'm sure my dad *could* find a way to sue her. But I don't know—that seems a little dramatic, don't you think?"

Ashley shrugged as she shielded her face with her hand so that the group of senior guys about to swagger by us wouldn't see her talking to me. "Okay, so maybe you don't *sue* her. But I bet our mom could make it so that she's banned from the prom because of this. I think I remember her talking about some Lifetime movie like this."

"And that way there'll be one less Jaden dress there!" added Britney.

"Thanks, guys." I sighed. "I'll think about it." So much for my theory about the Clones and compassion. This was all about the Jaden.

The last bell rang and everyone started to float into their classrooms. "Well, don't, like, go into the bathroom during lunch and hurt yourself over this or anything, okay?" said Ashley.

"Yeah. That would be kind of embarrassing," added Britney.

"Don't worry. I won't," I promised. I hoisted my book bag on my shoulder and marched to class. I wasn't embarrassed or ashamed—I was just *pissed*.

Seeing that it was my favorite subject, I had thought that English class would've made me feel better.

Ha.

As always, Ms. McManus's arrival was announced by the jingling of her Mexican silver bracelets. "Good morning, my darlings," she said as she twisted her long curly hair into a messy bun and secured it with a pencil. "So I was thinking that instead of spending the morning talking about the similarities between *Lord of the Flies* and *Lost,* we would talk about something a bit more apropos to today's current events." She clomped over to the blackboard in her clogs and picked up a piece of chalk and started writing.

When she was done, she stood back and beamed at us.

And Then They Lived Happily Ever After: How the Balls of the Fairy Tales of Yore Evolved into the Modern-Day Prom as We Now Know It.

"You're kidding, right?" I piped up from the back.

Apparently, from the confused look on her face, she wasn't.

"They've even brainwashed *you*, Ms. McManus?!" I asked, my voice rising. "You said you didn't even *go* to your prom!"

She nodded solemnly. "And then I spent the next ten years of therapy talking about it."

I shot out of my chair and started pacing. "See? That's *exactly* what I'm talking about!" I squeaked. "Our society has been making such a big deal about this stupid prom stuff that *generations* of people are scarred by it! And you know what? It's not the media that we should be blaming—the problem starts in our schools!"

Ms. McManus took a deep breath. "Okay, Cindy—that's enough." It was obvious she was trying her best to remain calm, but the rising anxiety in her voice made it sound like she had sipped in helium. "Please go back to your desk now."

"See? Just another example of the school system trying to silence me!"

158

"I said *now*," she warned, her voice wavering.

I stopped pacing. "I'm sorry, Ms. McManus—you know you're my favorite teacher and stuff, but honestly, I just have to tell you I'm really disappointed in you. I expected more from someone as cool as you."

What I *didn't* expect was to end up in Ms. Highland, the guidance counselor's office fifteen minutes later.

In the two years I'd been at Castle Heights, my drug-and-eating-disorder-free lifestyle had made it so that I had managed to avoid a trip to Ms. Highland's tribal-knickknack-covered office. Just as the nurse doled out Tylenol like they were Pez, Ms. Highland was under the impression that every kid at Castle Heights needed to be on antidepressants and would refer them to a Beverly Hills psychiatrist. When she showed up one day in a brand-new Mercedes instead of her beat-up Toyota, India decided that she had some sort of thing going with the pharmaceutical companies where she got a kickback every time a student cashed in his or her prescription for Zoloft.

I don't know if Ms. Highland was on meds herself, but she sure could've used an appetite suppressant. Every year her muumuus got larger and larger.

"Hello, Cindy," she said, brushing doughnut crumbs off a purple one that had an African vibe going on. Instead of sitting behind her desk, she pulled a chair up to the couch where I was sitting. "I'm *so* glad you're here. You know, I really think I can help you if you let me. Do you think you'd be willing to let me do that? Hmm?" I almost expected her to pull out a straitjacket.

I remembered an article I had read in my dad's *Newsweek* about how if you were ever a hostage, it was best to just agree with your captors.

"Sure. Why not?" I replied.

"Wonderful." She smiled. "Now, Ms. McManus filled me in on your outburst in class, and I was thinking the best way for us to deal with all your anger and hostility is for us to have a chat with Little Cindy."

"Who's Little Cindy?" I asked.

"Your inner child," she answered.

"Oh."

"You *do* talk to her on a regular basis, don't you?"

"Um . . . no?"

She grunted. If it were possible to shame someone to death with a look, I would have been six feet under.

"But I *have* been going to therapy for the last four years," I added. "Maybe you've heard of him—Dr. Norman Greenburg? From Gerstein Greenburg Gugliotta and Associates?"

She shook her head.

"Oh." So much for Dr. Greenburg's claim in his press kit that he was "world renowned." "Well, he's very good. He specializes in adolescent girls. My stepmother said that she heard that The N called him about putting him on retainer as their mental-health consultant for all their series."

Luckily, that seemed to impress her. "Interesting. Well, I have to say I'm surprised that someone of his stature doesn't have you dialoguing with your inner child, but that's okay—it's never too late to start. But we've got to get going. I'm meeting with Larry Goldfarb's parents in fifteen minutes to talk about his pyromania. So let's begin, shall we?" She closed her eyes, wiggled around in her chair, and took a very loud, deep breath. I wondered if it was going to be like a séance or something.

A moment later she opened her eyes. "What's the matter?"

"Uh . . . nothing," I replied. "I'm just not sure what I'm supposed to do."

For someone who was a guidance counselor, Ms. Highland sure didn't hold back with the looks of disapproval. It was like being around Clarissa. "Just close your eyes"—she sighed—"and go to your special safe place."

I closed them. And then I opened them. "Um, Ms. Highland?"

"*What*, Cindy?" she asked, eyes still closed.

"Do you mean my bedroom or something like that? Because other than that, I don't really *have* a special safe place. Well, I guess it could be the library . . . I like the Fairfax branch a lot—"

Luckily, for me *and* her, the bell rang. She leaned over and took my hands in hers. "Cindy," she said, "nothing would make me happier than to help you, but it's obvious that you've got some pretty big blocks against vulnerability and healing. So what I'd suggest is that you talk to Dr. Greenstein—"

"Greenburg."

"There's no need to make me an object of your hostility as well, Cindy—Dr. Green*burg*, about perhaps going on Zoloft for a while. Not only do I think it'll do wonders for you in those areas, but it will also help you with your anger and authority issues. Do you think you have enough self-love to participate in your own healing and give it try?"

"I'll think about it," I said. *Not.*

"Wonderful," she said. We both stood up. "And remember—my door is always open. For Little Cindy, or for Big Cindy."

I nodded and got out of there as fast as I could. Just like people said, "Those who can't teach, teach gym," it seemed that those who can't make it as shrinks end up as guidance counselors.

By lunchtime, I was no longer the "weird, antiprom girl," but had become "the weird, *violent* antiprom girl." Somehow the story had grown from me telling Ms. McManus that I was disappointed in her to me standing over her threatening her with Taylor McCrory's nail scissors.

I had to admit it was cool having kids look at me with newfound respect as I made my way outside to the lunch tree. Maybe I'd embrace my inner Jane Fonda circa 1969 and invest in a cool pair of thigh-high boots and become a rebel.

"Right on," yelled Wally Twersky as he stopped strumming his guitar to give me a thumbs-up.

"Thanks," I yelled back. With his new haircut (well, *only* haircut in about three years), Wally looked kind of cute.

"*Someone's* become a total flirt overnight," said Malcolm as I plopped down beside him and India and tore open my tuna-fish sandwich. Being the subject of school gossip made you really hungry.

"Yeah, well, you know—fame becomes me," I said between bites. "But, seriously, can we talk about something other than me, please?"

"How about we talk about the fact that you'd better wipe off the glob of mayonnaise on your cheek because Adam Silver's about to walk by with his friends in about two—"

Seconds. I looked up and there he was, in his post-soccer lunch glory. With a thin sheen of sweat on his forehead that, on anyone else, would have looked gross, but on him only added to his hotness.

"Hey," he said. It was obvious that his two friends Ian and Jake had no idea why they were stopping to talk to three low-life sophomores.

"Hey," I said, dabbing at my cheek, which, from Malcolm's expression, made me think I was spreading the mayo rather than wiping it up.

"So I hear you're now on the Castle Heights Most Wanted list." He smiled.

"Yeah, *20/20* called to see if they could get an exclusive interview." I smiled back.

I couldn't believe myself: I was actually kind of . . . *flirting.* From the looks on Malcolm and India's faces, I wasn't the only one who couldn't believe it.

I willed myself to rein it in. If Noah was my straight soul mate like I thought he was, it was imperative that I not do anything to screw things up just because my hormones seemed to go off the chart when I was around Adam Silver. I knew from TV movies just how dangerous lust could be. It started with some innocent flirting, but before you knew it, you were stealing away to cheap motels and planning someone's death for the insurance money.

"Dude, c'mon, if we want to get some chow before class, we gotta motor," said Ian.

"You guys go ahead. And get me a tuna-fish sandwich, okay?"

"Oh, wow—*Cindy's* eating a tuna-fish sandwich, *too*," announced India.

"That's so—"

"Not important," I said as I glared at her. I couldn't believe she had just broken commandment number 11: *Thou shalt not embarrass best friend in front of hot guy even if she's technically in love with someone else.*

Adam smiled at India and Malcolm. "We've never officially met—I'm Adam," he said.

"India," said India.

"Malcolm," said Malcolm.

I just *knew* I had been right about Adam being a nice person. What kind of senior not only stops to talk to sophomores when he's obviously starved because he just finished a grueling game of soccer to keep his physique in top form, but then takes the time to acknowledge said sophomore's best friends?

Adam nodded. "Nice to meet you. Nice shirt," he said to Malcolm.

"Thanks," said Malcolm. Because we were nearing the end of the school year, Malcolm had finally decided to stop dressing like a middle-aged investment banker and instead resembled a teenager, which explained the vintage *Fast Times at Ridgemont High* T-shirt. "So, Adam—obviously a lot of people are talking about Cindy nowadays, but, you know, that's not the only thing they're talking about . . . "

Because Malcolm was my best friend, I could read his mind, so I knew where he was going and I didn't like it.

"Oh yeah? What else are they talking about?" asked Adam.

"They're talking about the fact that *you* have yet to announce who you're taking to the prom."

He laughed. "Yeah, what's up with that? I mean, who cares who I'm taking?"

"Hmm . . . let's see . . . the whole student body?" Malcolm replied.

He had just broken commandment number 12: *Thou*

shalt not MORTIFY best friend in front of hot guy even if she's technically in love with someone else.

"You want to know who I'm taking?"

We nodded in unison.

"The truth is, I don't know who I'm taking. Maybe I'll follow Cindy's lead and just bag it completely and go . . . bowling or something."

He turned to me and gave me what appeared to be a wink, but probably wasn't, because why would Adam Silver be winking at *me*, especially after discovering that my so-called best friend had no boundaries?

"I gotta go. Nice talking to you. See you around, Cindy."

I managed to eke out a "Bye."

The three of us watched in silence as he walked toward the building.

Finally I spoke. "Excuse me, but was that a wink?"

"That was *so* a wink!" squealed Malcolm.

"Or did a piece of dust fly in his eye and he was trying to get it out?"

"No way," said India. "That was most definitely a wink."

I shook my head hard, as if I was trying to get water out of my ears. "You guys, I have to stop this."

"Stop what?" asked India.

"I'm an awful, awful person. It's like I'm cheating on Noah," I replied.

"Your *gay* boyfriend?" Malcolm snorted.

"I told you—he's *not* gay."

"Okay, well, has Noah winked at you?" he asked.

"No," I admitted. "But that's because he's an adult. And he knows that if you move too fast and start introducing the sexual stuff too quickly, the relationship is doomed for failure."

"Nice try," said Malcolm.

Having never received a wink before (at least not from a hot guy), I had no idea that it had so much power. I replayed the moment over and over the rest of the day—in chemistry, while Mr. Machado droned on about the importance of making sure we wrote our equations correctly or else we'd risk blowing up the school (the fact that Larry Goldfarb was scribbling notes was a bit alarming); during softball in gym class (which resulted in me missing every fly ball in center field and getting chewed out by first basewoman Jenny Norton, who took the game *very* seriously). Forget about Zoloft—all I needed was a wink from a sweaty senior with an incredible smile to rearrange my brain chemistry. Even having to sit at the dinner table while the Clones and Clarissa debated whether they should try and get Dakota Greene and her Jaden expelled from the prom didn't bother me—I just escaped to my special world of winks.

I could only imagine how much power a really great kiss would have.

However, I had a feeling that as cool as Adam Silver

had been that day, only someone as mature and well read as Noah would be able to truly "get" a girl like me. Call it that intuitive gift of mine, but I just knew that Noah could see my true essence.

As I was getting ready for bed, I couldn't control myself.

AntiPrincess: so i got winked at 2day.

BklynBoy: ur tutor?

AntiPrincess: nope. by my other crush.

BklynBoy: OTHER crush???

AntiPrincess: senior. name: adam silver. totally out of my league.

BklynBoy: how come?

AntiPrinces: a) senior b) most popular guy in school c) 90,000 other reasons

BklynBoy: hmm . . . sounds like prom king material

AntiPrincess: EXACTLY!!! except supposedly he hasn't asked anyone yet. I think it's just a front—he's probably going with a duff sis

BklynBoy: so what's he like?

AntiPrincess: um . . . PERFECT?

BklynBoy: LOL. sorry to tell you this, but no one's perfect.

AntiPrincess: i know, but he's close to it.

BklynBoy: what about yr tutor?

AntiPrincess: i'm seeing him thurs.

BklynBoy: so what do u like about him?

AntiPrincess: who?

BklynBoy: this adam guy.

AntiPrincess: oh. let's see . . . he's hot?

BklynBoy: gold, ur going way 2 LA on me. when did u get so superficial???

AntiPrincess: well, i guess i like that when he looks at me, it's like i feel that he sees me . . . it's like no matter how much of a dork i am—and BTW around him i'm a HUGE one—it doesn't freak him out . . . i don't know how to explain it, but it's like he sees past that . . . i feel like he knows me.

BklynBoy: he's lucky.

AntiPrincess: ?

BklynBoy: to get the chance to know u in person. wish i could.

AntiPrincess: are you flirting w/me??

BklynBoy: hmm . . . maybe. *yawn* i'm off. nite.

The permaloop of the wink was replaced by total confusion. For my first fifteen and a half years on the planet, my experience with guys had been so minimal that I would have probably been considered borderline retarded by most magazine quizzes. Then, within seventy-two hours, I found myself torn between three men. Okay, so maybe one of them possibly liked guys, and another may have had a speck of dust in his eye, and another lived three thousand miles away and I had no idea what he looked like, but still—the drama was just . . . *exhausting.* Which was a good thing, because the sooner I fell asleep, the sooner I could get up and go to school and see Adam Silver again. Not to mention the closer it would be to Thursday and my tutoring session with Noah.

chapter ten

One of the best things about having a shrink is that because they're being paid to listen to you, you can spend as much time as you want obsessing about something and not have to worry if you're boring them.

Which is why, instead of continuing last week's discussion about how it felt to be constantly invalidated by the woman who was supposed to be fulfilling the role of nurturance and unconditional love in my life (or something like that), I instead chose to spend the first forty minutes of my fifty-minute session on a monologue about the psychic pain of being torn between three men.

". . . and so, in summation," I said, wrapping up, "that's why I think that, ultimately, *Noah* is the best match for me. Especially since you're always saying how mature I am for my age. Don't you think so?"

No answer. Obviously Dr. Greenburg was giving the matter a lot of thought. That's why he was such a good shrink—he really *cared* about his patients.

"Uh, Dr. Greenburg?" I asked.

His eyes fluttered a few times, like my dad's did when he was done "resting with his eyes open."

"Right. And how did that make you feel, Cindy?" he asked. That was Dr. Greenburg's stock answer to most things I said.

"What? The wink? Or my decision to just give myself completely to Noah?"

"The wink; the shaming from your fellow students; the feelings of profound alienation that one often feels when taking the risk to be an individual in a society that glorifies the group-based mentality."

"Huh?" I said through my yawn. Listening to Dr. Greenburg always made me sleepy. I think it was because he spoke in such long sentences.

"Hmm. Interesting," he said as he made a note on his yellow legal pad. One night I was going to break in and find that pad so I could see what he *really* thought of me. "Cindy, I think that your obsession with all these boys who are in some way emotionally unavailable—"

"Noah's not a boy—he's a *man*. I told you he was twenty-three, remember?"

He ignored me. "—is just a coping mechanism to deal with the profound sense of grief and isolation that began when your mother died and has yet again been triggered by this latest trauma."

I yawned yet again. Dr. Greenburg liked to bring

everything back to my mother's death, which made no sense to me: the whole idea of therapy was to feel better—not worse. "Wait—okay, I get the unavailability thing, seeing that BklynBoy lives in New York, but why is *Adam* emotionally unavailable? I know you're the doctor here, but I'd say a wink basically screams 'I'm available!'"

"However," he continued, "if one is to individuate into one's true self, a certain amount of isolation is, in fact, necessary." He stood up and walked over to the bookshelf filled with such classics as *I'm Not OK, You're Not OK—And That's OK* and *Thin Is Not In: Size 8s Speak Out About Love, Sex, and the Joys of No-Guilt Ben & Jerry's* and took down a copy of *The Complete Fairy Tales of the Brothers Grimm.* "For instance," he said, settling himself back in his chair and flipping through it—past what I was sad to see was a hideous illustration of my namesake—"if we were to go back and analyze the great fairy and folktales of all time, we'd find that in almost every case, the heroines were cast out of their societies and forced to endure great hardships until their true worth was realized and they became princesses—"

Had *all* the adults around me gone completely insane?

"Enough with all this stuff about fairy tales!" I exploded. "I'm not some princess who lives in a faraway land full of moats and dragons and all that other junk— I'm a fifteen-year-old girl from L.A.! And you're a shrink!

You're supposed to be rooting me in *reality* here, Dr. G— not comparing my life to a stupid fairy tale where some dumb girl is rescued by a prince. I can take care of myself just fine, thankyouverymuch."

Dr. Greenburg stroked his beard and stared at me. I hated when he did that. It made me feel like a lab specimen. He nodded. I especially hated the head nodding.

"Hmm. Interesting." He nodded as he made another note. "I think that's all the time we have today, Cindy."

I had never been so excited—let me rephrase that: I had never been excited, *period*—to see Clarissa as I was that afternoon when she pulled up her usual twenty minutes late to pick me up. I was so relieved to be free of Dr. Greenburg's theories about why I found fairy tales so "threatening" that after I hoisted myself up into the Escalade, I impulsively reached out and hugged her bony body.

"Oh, my goodness!" she yelped once I let go. "What on earth was *that* for?"

And Dr. Greenburg wondered where I got my "aversion to bodily contact and demonstrations of emotion."

"Nothing." I sighed.

The good news about Clarissa is that she has the attention span of a gnat so unless it was gold circle status at Neiman Marcus presales, private lessons at the S Factor with Sheila Kelly to learn pole dancing, or something else that would benefit her, she lets things go pretty quickly.

She threw the truck into gear and peeled away from the curb. "So, sugar, as I was driving over here to get you, through absolute *gridlock*, mind you, seeing that your appointment just couldn't be at a worse time of day trafficwise," she said, narrowly avoiding the legless man in the wheelchair in the middle of the crosswalk, "I was thinking that since we had that wonderfully bonding makeup moment on Saturday, maybe you'd like to go to Saks and I'll buy you your *own* makeup."

"Oh." I didn't have the heart to tell her that I was over the makeup thing already. Too much work. Plus, if I was going to be a writer, it would help if I kept my sight instead of blinding myself with an eye pencil.

"It's the least I can do now that you're finally showing some interest in your feminine side. Plus, I'm out of moisturizer. And Evelin put yet *another* one of my La Perla bras in the dryer, so now it's just useless. And even though it's not till January, I really should start looking for shoes to wear to Huck and Larry's commitment ceremony because the dress I'm wearing is the *hardest* shade of chartreuse to match. So would you like that, sweetie? A continuation of our stepmother-stepdaughter bonding? Hmm?"

"Um, when?" I asked.

"Cindy Ella," she harrumphed. "Please don't try and manipulate me like that, honey. You *know* how busy my career as a domestic engineer is—especially with the prom happening in *minutes*. We're going now, or we're not going at all."

Which meant I would miss the start of the *South of Nowhere* marathon because I forgot to set the TiVo before I left for school that morning. Pseudo bonding with Clarissa or watching Spencer struggle with her lesbianic feelings for Ashley? That was a tough one.

"I have to say—I'm both very disappointed and shocked about your lack of gratitude, honey. It's so not like you," she chastised. "So do you want to go or not? Tell me now, so I know whether to get into the left lane."

"Sure," I replied, continuing my run of one-word answer replies. For someone who wasn't Jewish, Clarissa sure had the gift of guilt.

Off we went to Clarissa's Beverly Hills home-away-from-home: Saks Fifth Avenue. Nestled in between Neiman Marcus and Barneys New York, the three-block length of Wilshire Boulevard served as the spiritual center of the city for the blow-dried, hard-bodied, trophy wives in town. You know how sometimes on the news they show Muslims making pilgrimages to Mecca? It's kind of like that, but instead of poor women sweating underneath their burkas, it's rich women in air-conditioned Mercedes waiting for valets to take their cars.

The minute we got inside, Clarissa marched me over to the Lancôme counter.

"Cindy Ella, I'd like you to meet Annette, one of my dearest friends," she said.

Annette's pencil-thin eyebrows shot up. "This isn't the *stepdaughta*, is it?" she gasped in her Queens accent. "Clarissa, you never mentioned she was . . . *gorgeous!*"

She grabbed my face and started molding it like it was Play-Doh. "Lookit these cheekbones!" she squealed. "Christi!" she barked to the Estée Lauder girl across the way. "You gotta get over here and lookit these cheekbones. They're *in-cred-a-ble!*" She swiveled my face so I was face-to-face with *her* cheekbones, as well as her mile-long eyelashes and ruby-red lips. With her jet-black hair pulled back into a tight bun, she looked like the nonanimated version of the Wicked Queen from Disney's *Snow White*.

Clarissa looked as confused as the group of Japanese tourists over at the Chanel counter.

Christi—more of a blond, Glinda the Good Witch type—used her pale pink-tipped fingers to examine my pores. "What great skin. How old are you, honey?" she drawled in a Southern accent.

"*Mmfifnnn*," I replied. It didn't matter whether models were dumb or not—if so many people poked at them like this, it wasn't like they could talk anyway.

"She's fifteen," said Clarissa. "People are *always* saying that even though we're not related, we look *so* much alike."

"Hmm. I don't see a resemblance," said Annette. She let go of my face and undid my ponytail. "I gotta tell you, kiddo—earthy beauty like this? In this town? Fuggedaboudit. You gotta boyfriend, sweetie?"

177

"Cindy Ella?" hooted Clarissa. "Other than the one time *I* got involved and fixed her up with a very nice boy who she said wasn't 'smart enough,' she's never even had a date!"

Annette pushed me down into a chair and started pulling out various tubes and jars. "Just you wait, honey—when I'm done with you, that little Lindsay girl and Nicole Whatshername—the skinny one—will be fightin' for your rejects."

Now that I was in the hands of someone who knew what she was doing, the wonderful world of makeup was a whole new experience. It was almost . . . *relaxing*. As Annette worked on me, a queasy look came over Clarissa's face, like she had eaten tofu that was past its expiration date.

"What's the matter?" I managed to get out as Annette applied some very gooey gloss to my lips.

"Nothing," Clarissa replied. "You just look so . . . "

"*Gor-geo-ous*, doll face!" trilled Annette as she thrust a mirror in my hands. "Here, look."

I barely recognized myself. My eyes were so much . . . *bigger*. And . . . *greener*. And my mouth—well, it may have felt like there was Elmer's glue on it, but it looked so . . . *kissable*!

"Wow. I . . . thank you *so* much, Annette. I look . . . *wow*. But—"

"But what, honey?" she asked. "You think I went too

heavy with the Sultry Sable liner? 'Cause that's easy enough to tone down—"

"No." I sighed. "That's not it. It's just . . . I'm never going to be able to do this myself."

"Don't worry, sugar—that's exactly what stepmothers are for," Clarissa said, patting my arm. "And I'm going to help you every step of the way," she bravely announced.

It was like we were starring in the Lifetime Original Movie *From Humdrum to Hottie: The Cindy Ella Gold Story.* I have to admit: it was nice to have Clarissa look at me with respect and—dare I say it—a little bit of jealousy rather than her usual "how'd I end up with *this* for a stepdaughter?" bafflement.

"Clarissa?" I asked.

She handed her platinum Amex card to Annette. "It's fine, honey. I know how grateful you are. It's my pleasure, really."

"Actually, what I was going to say—I mean, in addition to thank you, obviously—was that I was wondering if maybe we could look around in the juniors section for a second after this." As long as the Amex card was already out, there was no reason it couldn't be used for a new outfit for Thursday's tutoring session. Especially since *Operation Turn Cindy into a Girl* was back in full swing. Malcolm would be so bummed he wasn't here—shopping is *always* more fun when you're using someone else's money.

She looked up from signing the receipt and beamed. "Of course we can! Oh, honey—I have *never* felt closer to you than I do at this moment." She squeezed my hand. "Let's go."

It turned out that, unlike Macy's, Saks didn't have a juniors department. They had what they called the contemporary department. And it sure didn't have juniors' prices.

I couldn't help myself. "A hundred and eighty-eight dollars for a dress made out of a towel?!" I squeaked as I peered at the price tag on a burnt sienna (to me, it was ugly orange) Juicy Couture terry minidress.

The salesgirl—who was so skinny that she could have gotten away with the washcloth version of the dress—looked like I had just taken off my clothes and started doing cartwheels through the aisles.

"Cindy Ella!" hissed Clarissa. "Stop that right now. Just go wait in the fitting room and I'll bring in some cute things for you to try on it."

I did as I was told—not because I trusted Clarissa's sense of style, but because being around so much "cute" was already making me nauseous. I had just gotten comfortable in the overstuffed fitting-room chair when Clarissa and Washcloth Girl click-clacked in with enough skirts, dresses, and tank tops of the white trash variety to dress Britney Spears for the next fifty years.

"You're kidding, right?" I asked.

"Everything we've brought you is currently in either *Lucky, Elle,* or *In Style,*" sniffed Washcloth Girl. "And this one," she announced, holding up a denim halter dress that had *Kiss My Grits* stitched in gingham on the butt, "is what Jessica Simpson is wearing on the cover of *Angeleno* this month."

If Clarissa had saved anything from her trailer-park days, she could've topped the Best Dressed list this season.

I knew she wasn't going to let me out of there without buying *something,* so a half hour later, I was the proud (at least that's the vibe I tried to give off) owner of a new denim miniskirt ("Who knew you had such fabulous legs?!" trilled Clarissa as I, and my seven reflections, modeled it for her) and a T-shirt (I drew the line at tank tops even though Washcloth Girl tried to convince me that double A's were all the rage this season) that said NASCAR WIDOW.

"Now that we've spent all this time on *you,* Cindy Ella, I'm just going to take two minutes to poke around for myself, okay, honey?" Clarissa said.

Two minutes turned into fifteen turned into a half hour turned into an hour. By the time we got to lingerie, I was sure I had slipped a disc from carrying her bags.

While Clarissa poked through bras and other lacy items that looked like they could cause death by itching, I wandered over to a chaise lounge across the way in the dress department and plopped myself down. There was something to be said for shopping at stores that were more high end than The Gap. It was so comfy I could've taken a nap.

Fantasizing about how good an Uncle Eddie's Vegan Chocolate Chip cookie would taste at the moment, I watched Clarissa examine a black lace thingy that looked like it belonged on the body of someone much younger. I shuddered—the idea of her wearing something like that in front of my dad was just . . . *wrong.*

"Looking for a prom dress?" I heard a voice say.

I looked up to see a saleswoman with a bob that looked like it wouldn't move in a hurricane.

Lack of food and so much estrogen had me more than a little cranky to begin with before having to deal with *that* issue again. I forced myself to breathe from my core. "No. Just waiting for my stepmom."

"Because *this* would be *divine* on you," she said as she held out a silk minidress with thin spaghetti straps. It was the perfect shade of ripe, juicy, organic heirloom tomato red—which happened to be my favorite color. While it wasn't va-va-voom low-cut sexy, even on the hanger, you could see that it could turn someone with a boyish figure (read: me) into a sex goddess. Not to mention—I saw as I looked at the label—it was Prada, which would earn the Malcolm seal of approval.

I reached out and touched it. It was softer than Sushi after he got home from the groomer. I glanced at the price tag. "Twenty-five hundred dollars?! You've *got* to be kidding, right?" I yelped as I let go of it. I figured if I smudged it, I was looking at at least $150 in damages. "Do people really spend this much on clothes, or do you just give them away to movie stars and stuff? Because that much for a piece of clothing—even if it *is* red and really soft—is insane. That's, like, two months' worth of rent in New York!"

The Bob tried to hold back a laugh (I had a feeling that laughing was a no-no in the Saks Fifth Avenue Employee Handbook) and leaned in. "You want to know something?"

"What?"

"I agree with you," she whispered. "But I also have to tell you—once you go Prada, you don't go back."

"Ooh, how *darling*!" Clarissa squealed from behind me as she yanked the dress out of my hands and held it up to herself. "This would be so perfect for Maureen and Monica's commitment ceremony in March! But we should get going, honey. You know, there are other members in this family than just you."

I petted the dress one more time. "Well, bye," I said to The Bob.

"Bye." She winked at me.

I got home to an iMix waiting for me from BklynBoy full of Bob Dylan and Damien Rice and Alexi Murdoch and Bright Eyes. Lots of songs about how a good woman was hard to find. As much as BklynBoy may have been my Harry, the timing of him passive-aggressively letting me know I might be his Sally couldn't have been worse. Not when I was already madly in love with Noah and madly in lust with Adam Silver.

AntiPrincess: thx for the tunes.

BklynBoy: yr welcome. how was yr day?

AntiPrincess: good. clarissa took me shopping.

BklynBoy: for prom dresses? ;)

AntiPrincess: no. but I did see this one dress . . . i think anyone would look good in it. even me.

BklynBoy: i'm sure you'd look better than good in it.

AntiPrincess: how r u?

BklynBoy: okay. but I think I'm coming down w/ the flu or something.

AntiPrincess: bummer. if u lived here, i'd bring you chicken soup.

BklynBoy: & ginger ale?

AntiPrincess: of course. & popsicles. & if you were REALLY sick—a black & white cookie.

BklynBoy: LOL. thx. i'm going to bed. nite.

AntiPrincess: nite. feel better.

Maybe one day I'd have a reason to wear a little red dress. And maybe even a date to go with it.

Somewhere between when I went to sleep and when I woke up, it became clear that if I *did* want a date—like with, say, Noah—it was going to take more than a new outfit and some makeup to get me one.

The next day after school, instead of going home and watching *Oprah*, I had India drop me off at the Fairfax branch of the Los Angeles Public Library.

"Miss Swenson?" I whispered.

She stopped reshelving *The Power of Now* CDs and turned to me.

"Hi, Cindy. How are you?" She smiled. Maybe the fact that I knew all of the librarians at my local Los Angeles Public Library branch explained my lack of a social life.

"I'm fine . . . but I was wondering if you could help me." I leaned in so that the bag lady with the Mohawk examining the *Mantras for Abundance* CD down the row wouldn't be able to hear me. "I'm looking for some stuff about how to . . . deal with the opposite sex," I whispered.

She pulled out a CD and handed it to me: *From the Glass Ceiling to the Sky: How to Rocket Yourself out of a Repressed Patriarchal Society into the Fourth Dimension of Equality.*

I wasn't exactly sure what that meant, but I was pretty sure it wasn't going to give me any flirting tips.

"Um, actually, I was looking for something more about how to . . . *get a guy.*"

"Ohhh," she replied. "Well, then—follow me."

It turned out that underneath her mismatched clothes (and the Clones thought *I* had no style) and Coke-bottle-thick glasses, Ms. Swenson was a total seductress. Well, at least she had *read* about how to be a seductress. She soon had me settled at a carrel surrounded by *Men Are from Mars, Women Are from Venus; The Rules; The Real Rules: How to Find the Right Man for the Real You;* and my personal favorite, *Mama Gena's School of Womanly Arts,* which I remembered seeing on India's parents' bookshelf.

An hour later, between the rules and suggestions and positive affirmations, I thought my head was going to explode.

Rule #1: Be a creature unlike any other . . . when a relationship doesn't work out you brush it away so that it doesn't smudge your makeup and you move on.

But what if you kept finding out that you didn't know how to *apply* makeup?

Rule #5: Don't call him and rarely return his calls.

That one wouldn't be so hard to follow seeing that I didn't even have Noah's number.

When the Martian is in his cave, don't try and get him to come out.

Seeing that I had no idea where my Martian lived, that wasn't a problem, either.

"How's it going?" Ms. Swenson asked.

I looked up from my flip-flop, where I was writing crib

notes for tomorrow's tutoring session. "This is harder than studying for the SATs," I replied. "Not to mention the fact that all these people contradict each other. For instance, you have Ellen and Sherrie from *The Rules* saying don't call him, but then there's Mama Gena, who says to 'expose what you truly feel.' Okay, but what do you do if what you truly feel like is *calling* him to tell him how you truly feel?"

She thought about it. "Hmm. I'm not sure about that one." She picked up *Seductress: Women Who Ravished the World and Their Lost Art of Love*." This one's my favorite. Maybe there's something in the Cleopatra chapter that speaks to that."

"But I don't think they had phones back then," I replied.

She stopped flipping. "I guess you're right, but it can't hurt to check it out. Let me know if you need any more help, Cindy." Ms. Swenson headed back to her desk, and I turned back to my flip-flop.

Once I had covered every square inch of both flip-flops with words of wisdom, I jotted down the mantras from *True Love: A Practice for Awakening the Heart* on the back of my French homework and called it a day.

Even though I checked out *Why Men Love Bitches: From Doormat to Dreamgirl* in case I had insomnia, it turned out sleep wasn't a problem that night. The songs on BklynBoy's iMix were so beautiful that I was out like a light in no time.

chapter eleven

"*That's* what you ended up buying at one of the most highly respected department stores in the country?" asked Malcolm when I walked into French class on Thursday wearing my new miniskirt and my NASCAR WIDOW tee.

"The saleslady said it's like *the* look of the season," I replied. "Apparently it's in all the magazines."

"Maybe *Country Music Weekly*," he sniffed as he went back to sneaking glances at the *People* magazine he had hidden in his notebook.

Malcolm's lack of approval didn't help my mood, nor did the humidity. By lunch, my hair was so out of control that I belonged in the Jew-'fro Hall of Fame. It was a good thing that Adam Silver was out sick for the second day in a row because if what happened between us had indeed been a wink, I didn't want to risk having him regret it. Then, to make things worse, when India and I went into the bathroom after school so she could do my makeup before my tutoring session, I realized I had grabbed the floral makeup bag that held my maxi pads instead of my mascara.

"Maybe this is Goddess's way of telling you that you're beautiful the way you are and don't need to use products that have been tested on animals to change the way you look," she suggested.

"Maybe this is what I get for listening to Bob Dylan's 'Just Like a Woman' five times in a row this morning and trying to figure out the hidden meaning of why BklynBoy put it on the iMix he sent me," I replied. "Now what am I going to do?"

"I've got it! I have an idea . . ." India said.

A half hour later we were at Larchmont Beauty Supply. "Excuse me—ma'am?" India tried to get the attention of the woman behind the counter. When she didn't answer, because she was about eighty and in the middle of a nap, India tried again. "Excuse me! We have a Beauty 911 here!" she yelled.

The woman opened her eyes. "Okay, okay. You want to know what a Beauty 911 is? A Beauty 911 is when you're the head makeup artist for *Dynasty* like I was and you have to deal with both Joan Collins *and* Heather Locklear on a daily basis. *That's* an emergency. I'm Esta. So what can I help you girls with?"

"Well, Esther, my friend here—"

"Esta! Not Esther—*Esta!*" the lady yelled.

"Um, okay, Esta. My friend here is about to go meet with the guy who might end up being her soul mate—that is, if he's not gay—and it turns out that by mistake she forgot her makeup, so we were wondering, since you don't seem to be all that busy, if you might be able to use all the tricks you've learned over the years to give her a makeover so that she looks just as much like a goddess outside as she is in the inside. But you have to be fast because she has to meet him in fifteen minutes."

Esta's eyes narrowed. "You kids think I'd do something like that for *free*?"

India shrugged. "Well, yeah. Think of it as good karma."

She rolled her eyes. "Great. Another yogi. Listen, kids, seeing that my stories aren't on for another few minutes, I'm willing to help you out—but I don't do charity work. You gotta actually *purchase* the stuff. Do you have any idea how high the rents on this street are?"

Seeing that I was desperate, with fourteen minutes and counting, I grabbed a basket and ran through the aisles, throwing in whatever looked to be hottie-in-training-appropriate.

"Here," I said, dumping it out on the counter in front of Esta. I rummaged through my wallet and threw my "in case of emergency" Visa card down. If this wasn't an emergency, what was?

While India supervised ("Turquoise eye shadow may have looked great on all of Charlie's Angels back when you were working on the show, but I kind of think it clashes with Cindy's eyes"), I prayed that Esta and her shaky hand wouldn't stab me in the eye with the liquid eyeliner wand.

When the alarm on Esta's watch started beeping loud enough to wake the dead, she dropped the blush brush and scurried over to turn on the television next to the cash register.

"I've been watching *General Hospital* since it started in 1963. Never missed an episode and not going to start now," she said.

I picked up a mirror, even though I knew that the fact that India was doubled over in the corner with a strangled giggle escaping from her mouth every few seconds wasn't a good sign.

The makeup was so slick and shiny, I looked like a child-beauty-pageant contestant. "Um, Esta, do you have a bathroom I can use?" So much for waiting until Noah and I were a couple to go back to my fresh-faced makeup-free look.

Bare-faced and forty dollars poorer (or, rather, my dad was), I sprinted over to Café du Village, relieved to find that Noah wasn't there yet. I walked over to Gilles, who was standing up front.

"Hi, Gilles," I said. "I need a table for two, and since I'm looking for a little privacy, something in the back garden would be just lovely."

"Where eez Mademoiselle India?" he asked.

"She's on her way to Whole Foods to check out the Raw Foods Extravaganza," I said.

"Hmmph," he harrumphed as he led me back to the patio. In the way that only the French can pull off, all the plants and flowers had been "casually" placed in such a way that it looked like a set from a HGTV show. If it weren't for the deafening noise of the jackhammer from the bank parking lot next door, you would've thought that you were in the Loire Valley instead of Los Angeles.

"Gilles," I said as I settled into my chair. "When my guest arrives—his name is Noah, by the way—please send him back." I flashed a smile. "And I'd love an iced tea while I'm waiting."

He grunted, and although I may have just been being paranoid, I could have sworn I saw him sneer as he walked away. I made a mental note to spend my junior year of college in Rome rather than Paris.

I looked down at my flip-flop to do some last-minute cramming, only to find that the ink had blurred to the point where other than "seduce" and "manipulate," my notes were unreadable.

I looked up at the sky. *Are You there, God? It's me, Cindy,* I thought. *Listen, I don't have a lot of time because Noah's going to be here in, like,* seconds, *but I wanted to give You a quick shout out and say that I could really use Your help with the flirting stuff. So if You could possibly take a break from the Middle East and pop on over here to Larchmont Boulevard and give me some pointers as to what to say, I'd really appreciate it. Thanks. Oh, and if You could make my hair a little straighter, that would be awesome.*

Just then an unsmiling Gilles hustled a smiling Noah into the garden. If I had remembered how cute he was, there was no way I would have spent all that time and energy thinking about Adam Silver.

"Don't you look pretty," he said as he settled into his chair. "I just love your sense of irony with your T-shirts."

I would've preferred something along the lines of "You're so beautiful that I can't imagine not staring into your eyes every day for the rest of my life," but being called "pretty" by a hot guy was definitely cause for serious celebration. I wracked my brain to try to remember what rule talked about how to respond to a compliment, but came up blank. "Thanks," I replied. I willed myself to say something witty and charming. "Would you like some bread?" I said as I pushed the breadbasket toward him. "It's really good. Like the best in the city."

"No thanks." He patted his flat stomach. "I'm trying to lay off the carbs for a while."

How many times had I heard Malcolm say that *very* sentence? I could feel the blood drain from my face.

"But who am I kidding? The fries here are to die for," he said.

"Oh my God—I'm always saying the *same* thing!" I said. It was weird how connected we were.

"If I break down and order some, will you share them with me?"

"Okay." I blushed. If he was *really* gay, he would've had more willpower.

Gilles came by and took our order with a sneer. Noah looked around the room. "I always forget how cute it is back here. On HGTV last week they had something about turning your urban dwelling into a French country garden. I TiVo'd it, but I haven't had a chance to watch it yet."

I started gnawing at a cuticle. *It doesn't mean anything,* I thought to myself. *Lots of people enjoy HGTV.* Maybe he was just highly metrosexual. However, once our fries came and we finally got down to work, I found myself looking for every possible opportunity to use the advanced reading comprehension and vocabulary words to do some sleuthing about Noah's personal life so that I could put to rest the growing fear that Malcolm's vicious lies were not, in fact, vicious lies but were, instead, true. Unfortunately, it's difficult to find a way to work in "So do you like girls, or do you play for the other team?" when you're discussing the pioneers of astronomy.

Finally I found my in.

The word was *cohabitation.*

"So . . . do *you* 'cohabitate' with anyone?" I asked in what I hoped was a seductive voice.

"I do. His name's Craig. We met up at Berkeley." Noah grabbed a fry.

"Ah. So you have a *roommate*."

He laughed and took a sip of his iced tea. "I guess that's what you'd call it if we were living in the 1950s or something. Obviously we're too young to think about making it legal, but we're definitely committed to each other."

My eardrums were shattered by the sound of my heart exploding into thousands of little pieces. "So you're—"

"Gay?" He nodded. "Yeah," he said nonchalantly as he reached for another fry.

Not only was he gay, but he was *insensitive* to boot. How could he stuff his face at a moment like this? Was he not aware of the fact that he had probably just scarred me for life? At least I could drop the Angelina-in-training act and stop arching my back in my attempt to make it look like I had some boobage—that was the good news. The bad news was that even though there had been a lot of low points over the last few weeks, this one took the cake.

Of *course* Noah was gay. To have him be straight and fall in love with me back would have been too easy. I guess I knew in my heart of hearts. And I also knew that, as Dr. Greenburg was always pointing out, I was "stubbornly intent on getting the aspects of the outer world to fit my inner-world fantasies," but was it so wrong to want *something* to work out for me once in a while? It wasn't like I was asking to win a Pulitzer Prize in my twenties—all I was asking for was a boyfriend. Was that such a big deal?

I just want someone to hold hands with during John Hughes double features at the New Beverly and not get grossed out if he takes a lick of my ice-cream cone. Someone to speak in silly voices with, and share my iTunes library with, and let him put his hand in the back pocket of my jeans (but not while we are walking anywhere we might run into people we know because I still think it's cheesy). Someone who I feel like I can be one hundred percent myself with and he'll love me because of—rather than in spite of—my weirder quirks.

All I want is a best friend whom I can't wait to kiss again.

Instead I fell for the most unavailable of the un-availables—a gay man. But who could blame me? They are so much funnier and such better listeners than straight guys.

"Are you okay?" said Noah with concern. "You look a little pale."

I stood up. "Actually, I feel kind of weird all of a sudden. Like maybe I'm coming down with food poisoning or something." I started walking toward the door. "I'll just see you here on Saturday, okay?" I yelled over my shoulder so that he couldn't see the tears that were beginning to well up in my eyes. But I knew the truth—our relationship, both professional and personal, was over for good. There was no way I'd be able to face him again.

"Do you want me to drive you home?" I heard him call after me.

"No," I answered. "I'll be fine." Yet another lie. "I have a feeling that the throwing-up part won't start until I get home."

"Cindy."

I turned around. I figured I was far enough away from him that he wouldn't be able to see that I was crying.

"This isn't . . . because I'm *gay*, is it?" he asked quietly.

Well, it *was*, but not in the way he thought. "Of course not. My best friend in the entire world is gay. I love gay men. That's part of my problem."

His big blue eyes got even bigger and he turned red. "Ohhh. I see. Well, if it's all right, I'm going to call you later to check on you, okay?"

I shrugged. "Whatever," I said before walking away. Before I got to the door I turned back to get one last look at him. "Good-bye, Noah," I whispered like a heroine from a TV movie.

"You're *sure* you don't want me to drive you?"

I nodded.

"Okay. I'm really sorry you're not feeling well, Cindy. Really sorry. I'll check in later."

I put my hand up and gave one last wave. If I were

really brave, I would've broken out into "And I'm Telling You I'm Not Going" from *Dreamgirls* in a last-gasp effort to change his mind, but over the last few weeks I had drained my courage.

I was tapped out.

No wonder there are so many songs about how painful it is to get your heart stomped on. You have to do *something* with all those feelings. That, or numb out with a wide selection of candy from Rite Aid, which is what I was doing when Noah called two hours later to check in on me. I didn't answer, nor did I respond to his e-mail. Frankly, I was too depressed to do anything other than lie on my bed and stuff my face while I listened to my "Heartbreak Hymns" iPod playlist.

Thankfully, Malcolm didn't gloat too much when I called him and India to fill them in on what happened. He only said "I told you so" twice during the conversation, and spent the rest of it trying to cheer me up by saying that having my heart broken would make my writing that much better down the line. India spouted lots of her fortune-cookie yoga sayings—things like "Only by clearing out the clutter of the closet of your heart can you make room for the good stuff"—and although most of it went over my head, it still made me feel better. Even if I ended up going through life never having a boyfriend, at least I had them.

I was tearing open my second York Peppermint Patty when BklynBoy IM'd.

BklynBoy: wat up?

AntiPrincess: nothing. just gorging on sugar.

BklynBoy: uh oh—what happened?

AntiPrincess: turns out the tutor is GAY.

BklynBoy: ouch.

AntiPrincess: um, YEAH.

BklynBoy: sorry to hear that. kind of.

AntiPrincess: ??

BklynBoy: also kind of glad.

AntiPrincess: ???

BklynBoy: less competition now. i'm off. feel better. x

Before I could even respond, he was gone.
"X." Was that a kiss? Or just a typo?

chapter twelve

The next day, I stayed home from school. Luckily, Clarissa was too busy trying to get out of the house for a day of beauty maintenance to investigate my claim that I had a 101-degree fever. Sometimes a mental-health day can do wonders for your mood and attitude, especially when filled with a marathon of Nora Ephron movies where, despite a bunch of misunderstandings, everything ended happily ever after. Obviously my situation with Noah wasn't going to end happily ever after as I highly doubted he was going to come to the realization that we would have been the perfect couple. I even mustered the strength to reply to his e-mail and let him know I was doing okay. A day's worth of Meg Ryan had filled me with hope that somewhere there was indeed a lid for my pot.

By Saturday morning, I felt like a brand-new person. Or maybe I just felt like myself again, as evidenced by my decision to ditch my country-bumpkin-sexpot miniskirt look and show up for my tutoring session in my standard makeup-less, jeans, and T-shirt look. God, it felt good to return to my roots.

When I got to Café du Village, Noah was already there—along with a spread of croissants and *pain au chocolat*.

Although I could now focus all my crush energy back on Adam Silver (except for that cryptic X from BklynBoy), I couldn't help giving my hair one last smooth-over before taking a deep breath and heading over to the table.

"Hey," Noah said warmly as I sat down. Was it my imagination, or did his hair suddenly make him look really gay?

"Hi," I said back, focusing on the *pain au chocolat* instead of his eyes.

"Thanks for getting back to me yesterday. I was glad to hear you were feeling better. Sounds like it was a twenty-four-hour thing, huh?"

"Yeah. I guess so," I replied, still looking at the pastries.

It was quiet for a minute and then, calling on all the weeks' worth of work I had done in therapy on confrontation, I took a deep breath and looked him straight in the eye. "Noah, I've been giving this a lot of thought, and I think that if this has any chance of working, I need to be honest with you about something . . . "

"Sure. What's up?"

"Well, the thing is . . . I didn't have food poisoning. The truth of the matter is . . . IsortofhadacrushonyouandeventhoughMalcolmtoldmeheknewyouweregayhearingitfromyoustillreallyhurt."

"Sorry—can you repeat that? A bit slower this time."

Jeez—talk about putting salt in a wound.

"I said . . . over the course of us working together, I kind of developed . . . *feelings* . . . for you. Of, you know, the *romantic* kind. So when you told me you were gay . . . well, as you can imagine, it's not exactly what a girl wants to hear about the boy—sorry, I mean the *man*—she has a crush on."

He sighed. "I had a feeling that might have been part of what happened. Listen, Cindy, if I said or did anything to give you any sort of—"

I put my hand up. "Noah, please. If it's okay, I'd rather not talk about it anymore. I've given it a lot of thought, and I think that we can put this behind us and just go on as tutor and student." I sat up straight and put on what I hoped was a brave face. "At least I'm willing to give it a try if you are."

He nodded. "Absolutely."

"Good," I said, digging into the pastries. It turned out that confrontation made you really hungry. "So, uh, can I ask you a question?"

"Sure."

Even though there was no hope for us, I still waited

until I was done chewing to speak. "Did you ever used to date girls?"

He spread some raspberry jam on a croissant. "Yeah. Up until my junior year of college."

For some reason that made me feel better. It wasn't like I had been *completely* off the mark. He had only been gay for the last four years. Maybe I had been picking up on some leftover straight energy. I sighed as I popped the last of my *pain au chocolat* into my mouth.

"What's wrong?" he asked.

"Nothing. It's just that it's true what they say: all the good ones *are* gay."

He laughed. "I don't know about that, but I'm very flattered. Listen, I completely respect your desire to keep our relationship strictly tutor-student, but I'm going to say it anyway . . . when I *was* dating girls, you were exactly my type."

"Really?"

"Absolutely. Not only are you beautiful, but more importantly you're incredibly smart and funny. That's a rare combination—especially in this town."

I blushed and reached for a croissant. It turned out compliments made me hungry as well. "I think the 'beautiful' thing is pushing it," I said.

"I don't," he replied. "You know who you remind me of? Kyra Sedgwick."

"I've heard that before. My friend India loves her."

"And I happen to think she's hot."

"India or Kyra?"

"Kyra. I bet you have tons of guys after you."

"Hmm . . . let me think about that for a minute. Um . . . *no.*"

He laughed. I guess he really *did* think I was funny, because I seemed to be able to make him laugh a lot. "Any crushes? I mean, other than me, of course." He winked.

I looked at him and thought for a second. It *would* be nice to get an outsider's point of view on the Adam Silver situation—especially an older, wiser outsider. "Well, actually . . . there's this one guy. But it's a lost cause, so it's probably not even worth talking about."

"Why's it a lost cause?" he asked.

"Because he's a senior. And the most popular guy in school."

"Ah." He nodded gravely. "The whole upper-lower classmen thing. Got it. What's his name?"

"Adam Silver."

"You're kidding! I tutored him last fall! I *love* Adam!"

"You did?!" I squealed. If that wasn't yet another example of kismet, I don't know what was. "So obviously you get how crush-worthy he is," I said.

He nodded. "Obviously."

Now that the pressure was off to say and do all the right things to make Noah fall in love with me, I found myself spilling my guts and telling him the whole story, leaving out nothing—not even the maxi-pad explosion. Like Malcolm, he listened intently, occasionally asking a question in order to fully understand the situation.

"I mean, I like him so much that if he had asked me to the prom—which of course would *never* happen in a million years, I'm just using it as an example—I think I'd have to reverse my antiprom policy and go," I confessed.

"So no one knows if he's going?"

"Nope. But if he did, I bet he'll go with someone like Miley Cyrus," I said.

"Who's Miley Cyrus?" Noah asked.

"You know—Hannah Montana."

"Who's Hannah Montana?" the seminerd in him asked.

"The Disney Channel show?"

All I got was a blank stare.

"Never mind. Let's just say she's pretty famous. Not to mention way hot."

"So what are you going to do?" Noah asked.

"What do you mean? There's nothing *to* do. Graduation's in a few weeks and then I'll probably never see him again." Dr. Greenburg did a have point about me and the unavailable thing.

"Yeah, but I have a feeling you guys might really hit it off."

"You do?"

"I do. I definitely think it's worth exploring."

My phone beeped. *We're out front,* said the text from India.

"Shoot. My friends are here to pick me up," I said, gathering up my SAT book, which I hadn't even cracked open.

"Tell you what," he said as we stood up to leave. "I'm going to give this Adam thing some more thought and e-mail or call you about it later. Sound good?"

"Thank you *so* much," I said. I impulsively reached out to hug him. "Maybe I'll call you first? Being friends with someone who has so much life experience is going to be *so* cool."

Maybe the man of my dreams already had a man of *his* dreams, but at least I had someone who had actually been in relationships to help me get into one of my own.

If there was any question as to whether prom mania had taken over the city, you only had to go to The Grove—L.A.'s Vegas-ized version of a mall—that Saturday to see it in motion. Seeing that L.A. is the shopping capital of the world (not to mention a cultural wasteland), The Grove was always a madhouse on weekends; but I had never seen it this bad.

"You know, if just a quarter of the people here were home instead, writing their local congressperson an e-mail about that global warming bill, we'd have the environment cleaned up in no time," I said to India and Malcolm as a group of Clone clones almost pushed me into the synchronized fountain with their shopping bags.

Malcolm stopped in front of the Apple store and turned to me. "Excuse me, but I think I remember having you swear up and down on a pile of *Us Weekly*s that if you came with us, you'd behave yourself."

"I'm just making conversation."

"*No*, you're just being annoying. Why don't we just leave you here and come back for you in a few hours? You can . . . make an antiprom documentary or something with iMovie."

"The whole idea was for us to spend quality time together." I pouted. "Plus, there was no way I could've dealt with Clarissa and her Meditation for Dummies group today."

"You know, it makes me sick how people have warped the idea of meditation," said India. "It's not like it's some treatment you can sign up for at the dermatologist. It takes *years* to develop a practice."

"Maybe even lifetimes," I added.

"Oprah had it listed as one of her favorite things this month," said Malcolm. "She says meditation is the new Pilates."

Kool & the Gang's "Celebration" replaced Whitney Houston's "I Will Always Love You" on the mall's stereo system, which meant that the synchronized fountain's tempo revved into disco mode, which meant that because we were walking over the wooden footbridge that was supposed to make mall-goers feel like they were in some tropical beachfront village instead of a smoggy metropolis, we got soaked.

"What are they thinking switching from adult contemporary to dance music without giving us any kind of warning?!" yelled Malcolm.

"Now do you see why I hate this place?" I asked.

India crossed her arms in front of her wet T-shirt so that the group of eleven-year-old boys snickering over near the Hot Dog on a Stick cart would be forced to go elsewhere to feed their hormones. "Cindy's right—this is crazy. Plus, if my parents found out I got my dress at some mall store that used sweatshops, they'd kill me. Let's go somewhere else."

"Where?" I asked.

Malcolm smiled. "I know *exactly* where we're going."

After stalling twice during the twenty-five minutes it took us to get out of the parking lot, we were on our way to a place I had heard my father's family in Brooklyn talk about in the same hushed tone of voice they used when discussing the corned beef at Katz's Deli on the Lower East Side: Loehmann's. I'd never been—maybe if Clarissa had been Jewish instead of Jewish-by-third-marriage, I would have at least been left in the car in the parking structure there a few times, but Clarissa and her credit cards (well, my dad's credit cards) were strictly loyal to the trinity of Barneys, Saks, and Neiman's, and the boutiques of Robertson Boulevard.

"I'm telling you—Loehmann's is the new Kitson," announced Malcolm as we waited for a toupeed man in a convertible Mercedes to stop checking himself out in his side mirror and start moving. "Just last week in 'Stars—They're Just Like Us!' there was a picture of Paris coming out of the communal dressing room with a Helmut Lang dress."

"They have Helmut Lang?" asked an impressed India.

"Who's Helmut Lang?" I asked.

"Only *the* most important designer to come out of Austria ever. Of *course* they have Helmut Lang," Malcolm replied. "Haven't you heard about the Back Room? It's like the whole selling point of Loehmann's—huge designers at even more hugely discounted prices."

Not only did Loehmann's have Helmut Lang and huge discounts, but they had huge Russian women, and lots of them—both working and shopping there. It was like what I imagined the Saturday-morning marketplace in Moscow must look like.

"Ugh. It smells like someone took a bath in cheap drugstore perfume," whispered Malcolm as we poked around the Back Room. A saleswoman with triceps the size of ham hocks waddled past us carrying an armful of Armani. "Don't they realize they're contaminating the clothes?"

A red dress caught my eye. "Hey!" I said. "This is that

Prada dress that I saw in Saks the other day!" I looked at the price tag. "And it's only ninety-nine dollars and ninety-nine cents instead of twenty-five hundred dollars! Wow, you really *can* get great deals here."

Malcolm peeked at the label. "That's because it's a knockoff. Look at the label."

"Prodo. Oh. Well, it *looks* exactly like the other one."

"Yeah, except this one was probably made in bulk in Taiwan instead of lovingly handcrafted in Italy by a fourth-generation seamstress," sniffed Malcolm before marching over to check out the mountain of silk, satin, and chiffon India was struggling to carry around.

I stroked the silk, careful not to snag what passed for my fingernails on it. It felt like how I imagined my legs would feel if I could get over my fear of waxing. Whether it was Prodo or Prada didn't matter—the dress was beautiful.

Eau de Rotten Apples assaulted my nostrils and I turned around. "Ees bootiful, no?" asked a smiling Miss Ham Hocks.

"No. I mean . . . yes, is beautiful," I said as I put it back on the rack.

She yanked it back off and thrust it toward me. "Try on," she demanded. "You wear to prom and you look va-va-voom. Even with no boobies."

"I'm not going to the prom," I said as I picked up a leopard dress whose tag said Dolce & Gabbana. "My friends are. I just came along for the ride."

211

"But prom is big American holiday! Why you no go?"

"Long story. It's been nice talking to you, but I'm just going to go sit down on that bench over there—" Outside the dressing room, a row of bored-beyond-belief husbands and sons sat staring into space.

"No, you're not," said Malcolm, rushing over. "You're going to go keep India company in the dressing room." He grabbed the Prodo from Miss Ham Hocks and handed it to me. "Here, you can try this on so you don't feel like some sort of pervert."

"I tell her she look va-va-voom in zis dress!" said Miss Ham Hocks, "but she no care."

"Welcome to my world," sighed Malcolm.

Sick of the fashion intervention, I grabbed the dress and marched toward the dressing room. "Okay, okay—but I'm only doing this for India."

There were more half-naked bodies packed into the four-hundred-square-foot communal dressing room than would fill most of L.A. The way these women poured themselves into such skimpy dresses and paraded around the room gave new meaning to the phrase *let it all hang out.*

"What do you think?" India asked as she modeled a ruffled yellow chiffon gown.

She looked like a piece of lemon meringue pie. "Um . . . it's . . ."

"Hideous?" she suggested.

"Something like that," I agreed.

She examined the Prodo. "Ooh, this is beautiful! Are you going to try it on?" she asked. "Because if you're not, I am."

I yanked it back, wondering why I suddenly felt very possessive of my Prodo dress. "Yes, I'm trying it on."

I stripped down to my bra and underwear and gingerly stepped into it, careful not to rip the silk. It may have been only ninety-nine dollars, but that was about ninety more than I had to my name.

"Can you zip me up?" I asked India, who now resembled Violet Beauregard from *Willy Wonka and the Chocolate Factory* in a poufy purple dress.

After she zipped, she whirled me around. "Oh. My. God," she gasped.

"I look *that* dumb, huh?" I sighed, turning to get a look at myself in one of the mirrors.

"No. You look . . . incredible. Cin, it's like that dress was *made* for your body."

She wasn't half wrong. Even though it was made in Taiwan instead of Milan, the dress had a way of making everything that didn't work (i.e., my lack of boobies) work while making everything that did work (i.e., my long legs) work even better. Like the thinnest strands of spaghetti, the wisps of silk held the dress up, so that it looked like my body was floating in a red cocoon of cotton candy.

"Wow. So this is what I'd look like with curves," I

murmured as a few of my fellow Back Roomies began to ooh and aah in Russian. I felt like I had just been crowned Miss St. Petersburg.

India pushed me toward the exit. "You *have* to show Malcolm!" she screeched. "He's going to die!"

Before I knew it, I was putting on a one-girl fashion show for Malcolm, Miss Ham Hocks, and the rest of Loehmann's. "See?! I knew it!" announced Malcolm. "I *knew* that you could look like a model if you just made an effort!" After he was done dancing his little jig, he grabbed me by my shoulders. "Cindy Ella Gold—you are officially *babedacious*!"

I blushed. "Stop."

"You are. And you're so buying that dress. In fact, for ninety-nine dollars, India and I will buy it for you!"

"Okay, so it's gorgeous," I said. "But where am I going to wear it? The library?"

"Look, even if it's a knockoff, it's still classic. Something like that will never go out of style. You could wear it . . . to your book party when you publish your first novel. Or the Golden Globes when *Sixteen More Candles* is nominated for Best Musical or Comedy."

Unlike Clarissa and the Clones, who only needed the reason that it was Saturday (or Tuesday or Thursday) to buy something, it felt like a waste to me. I would have rather put the money toward something important, like a signed first edition of J. D. Salinger's *Franny and Zooey.*

214

But as I took one more look at myself in the dressing room before India unzipped me, I had to admit that I now understood why people were so into clothes. They could not only change the way you looked—they could also change the way you felt about yourself. And at that moment, I felt like the classiest, most beautiful fifteen-and-a-half-year-old in the entire city of Los Angeles. Which, in a town of freakishly beautiful people, was saying a lot.

That night, while I was watching a *Project Runway* marathon, my IM beeped.

BklynBoy: wassup?

AntiPrincess: watching project runway.

BklynBoy: YOU???

AntiPrincess: i know—weird, right? so malcolm & india made me try on a dress today.

BklynBoy: what kind of dress?

AntiPrincess: it was red. and kind of short.

BklynBoy: bet you looked smokin in it. so listen—i've been thinking—now that u have all these guys swarming u . . . want to be my un-prom date? we could not go 2gether.

AntiPrincess: LOL. sure. but u better leave a few days early to pick me up seeing that u live across the country.

BklynBoy: so it's a date?

AntiPrincess: LOL. sure.

History had just been made: I had been asked out on my first nonparental-fix-up date, even though he was obviously kidding. Between that and the dress, I guess *Operation Turn Cindy into a Girl* was working after all.

chapter thirteen

When I came down for breakfast Monday morning, I discovered that Clarissa had gone into full battle mode. She had a preprom spreadsheet schedule waiting for the Clones. Everything—waxing, spray tans, Pilates, mani/pedis, highlighting, haircuts, final fittings—had been scheduled to the minute.

"Wow, I didn't even know you knew how to use the computer, Clarissa," I said, flipping through her piles of paper. "These are really impressive." They could have used her in the military. The woman was a machine.

"Evelin helped me," she said, reaching behind the Clones' half grapefruits (according to the schedule, they were to have one half every two hours for the next five days—there was an article from the *Los Angeles Times* about the fat-burning properties of grapefruit attached to the spreadsheet) for another printout. "Here. I didn't want you to feel left out, so I made you one, too."

4:00–4:50 Tuesday	*Dr. Greenburg*	CEG to find own ride
3:00–5:00 Thursday	*Babysitting*	CEG to take care of SJG
3:00–5:00 Thursday	*Babysitting*	CEG to take care of SJG
3:00–TBD Friday	*Babysitting*	CEG to take care of SJG

"But what if I have stuff to do?" I asked.

"What could you possibly have to do, sugar, seeing that everyone you know is going to the prom?" she asked.

Sadly, she had a point.

By the time I got to school, the usual Monday Morning Blahs had turned to full-on Monday Morning Prom-Week Blahs. The fact that school was still in session was a joke. The teachers didn't even try to get anyone to focus on work—in fact, most of them were too busy hanging out in the teachers' lounge talking about what they were going to wear on prom night.

And then came the gossip.

For once, I wasn't the topic. Adam Silver was.

By third period, the halls were buzzing with the news that Jordan Goldman had heard from Alexa Miller, who had heard from her little sister, Tracy, who was best friends with Adam's sister Annabelle, that Adam had asked someone to the prom. He wouldn't say who his date was, but he had, indeed, confirmed to Annabelle that he was going.

I know I shouldn't have been surprised. And I definitely shouldn't have been as bummed as I was. But when I heard the news, I felt like the world's biggest balloon being deflated.

Now I had that Monday Afternoon Who-Am-I-Kidding-with-My-Crush-on-Adam-Silver Blahs. So what if he had sort-of-maybe winked at me? Adam Silver was as close to royalty as Castle Heights had. Of *course* he was going to the prom. That's what popular kids did— they went to the prom, and then they married their college sweethearts, and then they had kids, and then they got divorced and remarried. It was the American way.

Popular kids didn't spend their days walking around feeling like there was a How to Live Your Life manual that everyone had been given at birth, except them. They didn't spend their nights worrying about what happened when you died. They didn't spend their days and weeks fantasizing about how great it would be when they could finally leave their homes, where, if they weren't ignored, they got "constructive criticism" on how if they just changed everything about themselves, they'd be much better off.

I was never going to be popular. I'd be lucky if I didn't end up a shut-in with five cats, watching endless reruns of game shows. And a popular guy like Adam Silver was never, *ever* going to like someone like me.

I needed to talk to India and Malcolm. Thank God I had them, I thought as I waited for the cashier to ring up my tuna-fish sandwich that day. *If I didn't have them to talk to about deep stuff, like the meaning of life, I'd go insane.*

"Okay, so the bottom is like this really bright pink—" India was saying as I joined them under the lunch tree that day.

"Like fuchsia?" asked Malcolm.

"No. It's more like . . . "

"Salmon? Coral?" he suggested.

"Well, kind of like coral, but darker," she said. "And then the top is sapphire, but more . . . "

"Teal? Azure?"

Okay. Obviously any sort of meaning-of-life conversation was on hold for that day.

"What did you do? Study the Crayola box when you were little?" I asked Malcolm, as my daily glop of tuna fish fell on my IT'S ALL GOOD T-shirt.

He ignored me and turned back to India. "And where'd you get it?"

"This place called So Sari in Little India," she said.

"You're wearing a sari to the prom?" I asked.

"No. Her mom is doing a *Pretty in Pink* and taking a sari and sewing a dress for her! Isn't that *so* cool?" Malcolm sighed. "Okay, enough about you. So I was thinking that instead of a cummerbund, I would—"

While the two of them discussed whether they should grab something to eat beforehand ("Somehow I doubt they'll have a vegan entrée," said India) and if

Colin's dad's assistant had been able to track down a hybrid limo, I walked over to a different bougainvillea tree and pressed my newest speed-dial entry on my phone.

"Hello?" said Noah.

"Hi," I said. "It's Cindy. Is this a bad time?"

"Nope. Just avoiding writing. What's up?"

"A.S. asked someone to the prom," I whispered.

"Sorry—I'm having trouble hearing you."

"I said . . . A.S. asked someone to the prom," I said a little louder.

"What?"

"AmmmSilrr"

"Who?"

Maybe Noah wasn't gay, because there was no way a gay guy would be so clueless.

"Adam Silver!" I yelled, which prompted a group scowl from the Sylvia Plathites under the next tree.

"Ohhh . . . really. How interesting. Who'd he ask?"

"That's the thing—no one knows," I replied.

"Hmm. Well, why don't you ask him?" Noah suggested.

Noah may have been older, but he was definitely not wiser when it came to relationship stuff—in fact, he was kind of insane.

"Um, I don't think so," I said as the bell rang. "I have to go. I'll e-mail you later."

So much for Noah helping me win Adam's heart—someone else had beat me to the punch.

As the week went on, the blahs got worse and worse. It seemed like the stress level around town was rising faster than the smog index during the height of June Gloom. Maybe it was the greenhouse effect of a city full of girls doing some last-minute crash dieting, but if I could have stayed locked in my room until Saturday with a few bags of Uncle Eddie's Vegan Chocolate Peanut Butter Cookies and the complete third season of *The Hills* on DVD, I would've been happy.

Finally, the day of reckoning arrived. We technically had a half day on Friday so everyone could get ready, but other than me, the most Untouchable of the Untouchables, and India, who wasn't about to sabotage her perfect attendance record for anything, not even the prom, no one bothered to come. At 10 A.M. we were dismissed so that the teachers could get to their hair appointments on time.

"Are you sure you don't want me to wait for you?" India asked as we pulled up in front of Blockbuster on Larchmont.

"Don't worry about it," I said, wrestling with the door handle. "I know you have that lymphatic drainage massage at Burke Williams at noon." I hugged her. "I hope you have an amazing time tonight."

"After trying on those high heels last night, I'd much

rather stay home with you and Spencer and watch movies," she said. "Cin?" she said as Goldie Hawn's door finally popped open.

"Yeah?"

"I know how strong you are, but I'm going to bring my cell tonight," she said, "in case, you know, you end up breaking down or something and need to talk."

I gave her another hug. "Thanks. I appreciate it." The Universe may not have given me the world's most loving and supportive family or a boyfriend, but it sure made up for it when it gave me India and Malcolm.

Blockbuster was filled with hyper kids stocking up on various PG-13 movies instead of regular PG because it was a special night. Remembering what Dr. Greenburg had said in our Tuesday session ("I know you keep saying you don't want to go to the prom, Cindy, but I want you to be very gentle with yourself that night, in order to avoid post-traumatic stress syndrome"), I grabbed copies of *Valley Girl, Sixteen Candles,* and *Pretty in Pink* before stocking up on M&M's, Caramello bars, and Reese's Peanut Butter Cups.

Larry Goldfarb's older brother, Mark, was behind the counter. "So I guess you're not going to the prom," he said. Like Larry, Mark had served time in one of those juvenile Outward Bound programs. Now he was just a rehab retread.

"Um, I'm a *sophomore*?" I said. "And at least I'm still *in* school," I said, adding another Caramello bar to the pile. Like Dr. Greenburg said, it was important to be gentle with myself.

Then I grabbed a Mochaccino with extra caramel at the Starbucks next door, and amped up with sugar, I began what I hoped would be a very long walk home. The idea of being around Clarissa and the Clones for the next few hours sounded about as much fun as plucking the hairs out of my legs with tweezers.

As I finally made my way up the driveway, the wailing coming from the house made it obvious that however much down-to-the-minute planning that Corporal Clarissa had done, something had gone wrong. *Very* wrong. It sounded like they were filming the climax of *Sorority Babes Nail Scissors Massacre* in there.

"Oh, Cindy Ella! Thank *God* you're home!" said Clarissa as I walked in the front door.

The Clones were standing on the stairs in tears, wearing what I guessed were supposed to be their Jadens and showing even more skin than Christina Aguilera.

"What happened?"

"What does it look like?! The dresses are a disaster!" yelled Clarissa.

Disaster was an understatement. It turned out that a few nights earlier, Jaden had gone on the bender to end all benders and, in addition to losing her twelve years of sobriety, also lost her mind. The dresses she had come up with for the Clones in her drug-induced haze weren't exactly dresses . . . they were more like tattered rags that had been stitched together in various places.

Ashley's dress was all bunchy and missing a shoulder strap, while the other strap was so long that it kept falling off. At least it wasn't as bad as Britney's—her hem was cut on a wavy diagonal so that on her left side, it was a minidress, whereas on the right, a train of material dragged and drooped onto the floor. It was so long that Sushi could have used it as a bed, which is what he was doing at that moment. Apparently Jaden preferred the *au naturel* look—both dresses were fraying big-time along the edges. Obviously I wasn't an expert when it came to fashion, but even I could tell that these dresses were a nightmare. No wonder Clarissa looked like she was losing her mind.

Clarissa rummaged in her purse for her car keys and her Amex and threw them to me. "Here. I need you to go over to Saks and pick up every high heel in a size seven and a half you possibly can," she ordered.

"But don't get any Sergio Rossis," said Ashley through her tears. "They're too hard to walk in."

"What? Why do they need new shoes?"

"What do you mean why?! Because now that the girls are going to have to wear their original dresses, they don't have the right shoes!"

"But I only have my learner's permit," I protested.

"So just be extra careful—can't you see this is an

225

emergency?!" Clarissa shot back as she hustled the girls up the stairs.

"But I've only practiced on Dad's Mercedes!" I called up to her. "The Escalade is way too big for me. Can't I take the Saab?"

"The Saab is at the shop. You'll be fine," she yelled back.

I headed for the garage. Now I *knew* Clarissa had lost her mind—the fact that she was trusting me with her car was a sure sign of insanity. Trying to maneuver an Escalade wasn't just an accident waiting to happen—it was more like a death wish. I climbed in, took a deep breath, and turned the key.

"*Icandothis, Icandothis, Icandothis,*" I repeated over and over as I pulled out of our driveway, trying not to hit the fountain. Slowly, I inched down the street. My cell phone rang. It had to be Clarissa wondering where I was and why I was taking so long. I let it go to voice mail—I couldn't even dream of trying to talk and drive at the same time. But it just kept ringing. For most of the drive, a seventy-five-year-old man in a Cadillac slammed on the horn because I was doing twenty-five in a forty-five zone, and it almost gave me a heart attack. Finally, I made it to Saks. All I could say was thank God for valet parking. The idea of having to park that boat was more than I could handle.

The store was a madhouse. Worse than opening day of H&M. Mothers of high school girls across the city were in full battle mode, grabbing last-minute items they had forgotten: bronzer, Spankys, push-up bras with extra padding.

I headed straight for the shoes. "Hi," I said to the sales guy, who, according to his name tag, was Juan Carlos, assistant manager of the Saks Ladies Shoe Salon. "I'm looking for some shoes."

He gave me one of the raised eyebrow/nostril flares that Malcolm was so fond of, as he looked down at my flip-flops. "Mm. Yes. I can see why. So what are you looking for today? A mule? A slide? Ooh—we just got the most darling Chanel ballet flats in yesterday! Let me guess—you're a size . . . . seven and a half?"

"How'd you know?"

"It's my *job*," he sniffed.

"Impressive, but actually, the shoes aren't for me. They're for my stepsisters. For the prom. See, there was a screwup with their dresses—"

"Let me guess: Jadens," he said. "That woman just committed career suicide," he tsk-tsked.

I nodded. "They're both size seven and a half, too, and I don't even need to try them on." I held up Clarissa's Amex card. "I'm just going to buy them."

Even though I was sure I wasn't his type, Juan Carlos looked like he had just laid eyes on *his* soul mate. "I have a feeling you and I are going to become *very* good friends, Miss—"

"Cindy."

"Mademoiselle Cindy, I'll be right back."

I plopped down in an empty chair, and waited for Juan Carlos to return with the shoes, trying to stay out of the line of fire as women all around me fought over shoes. It was like watching *When Animals Attack: The Outtakes They Never Wanted You to See.*

"Cindy?" I heard a voice say.

I turned around to find Noah standing there with another seminerd hottie. This one had a mop of brown curls and black-rimmed glasses and was wearing an Elvis Costello T-shirt.

"Noah! What are you doing here?" I asked.

He pointed to the garment bag that the guy was holding. "We had to pick up Craig's tux for the mock prom at the West Hollywood Gay and Lesbian Center tonight. Craig, this is Cindy."

So this was my rival. For the second time in my life, I fell in love with a gay man. Craig was just as cute as, if not cuter than, Noah. Life could be so cruel sometimes.

Craig stuck out his hand. "It's so nice to finally meet you. Noah's been raving about you."

Not only was he hot, but he was sweet to boot. Plus his Southern drawl was so charming I was about to die.

"What are you doing here?" asked Noah.

I filled them in on the Jaden crisis, my shoe mission, and my terror-filled ride in the Escalade. "I don't know how anyone drives anywhere in one of those things!" I said. Just the thought of getting back in that car made my shoulders tense up.

"Would you feel better if I drove you back and Craig followed us?" asked Noah.

I felt my shoulders unhunch. "Gosh, that would be so great," I exhaled. "Are you sure it's not too much trouble?"

"Not at all. Plus, as your tutor, it's the least I can do. Somehow I don't think a college admissions committee would be too impressed by a police record."

Juan Carlos came staggering back with enough shoe boxes to take care of the Rockettes and dumped them on the floor. As he took the tops off the boxes, my anxiety returned.

I stared at the sea of heels and turned to Noah and Craig. "Um . . . *help*?"

Thanks to the kindness and fashion sense of my ex-soul mate and his current soul mate, twenty minutes later, a grinning Juan Carlos rang up fifteen pairs of Jimmy Choos, Pradas, Manolo Blahniks, Guccis, and Christian Louboutins for $5,243.45. No wonder he was happy; that was a pretty sweet commission.

I glanced over my shoulder at Noah and Craig and handed over Clarissa's Amex with a smile. I was starting to understand how addictive it could be to use a little plastic card to buy whatever you wanted.

The drive home was a lot more relaxed with Noah at the wheel. Not to mention a lot faster at regular speed instead of old-people speed.

"That's cool that the Gay and Lesbian Center is having a prom," I said as we zoomed down Wilshire.

"Yeah. To be honest, I kind of feel the same way about proms as you do, but since Craig didn't go to his high school one, I wanted him to be able to experience it."

"But how come he didn't go the first time around? He's a total fox."

"Let's just say that six years ago, the good people of Charleston, South Carolina, probably wouldn't have taken too kindly to two guys showing up together on prom night. So what are you going to do tonight?" he asked.

I shrugged. "Watch some movies. Eat a lot of sugar. Basically the same thing I do every Friday night."

"Hmm. Well, maybe you'll get a surprise invitation or something," he said.

"Seeing that everyone I know will be at a prom— including you—I highly doubt it. Plus, I'm babysitting Spencer."

"You never know. They don't call prom night 'magical' for nothing, you know."

I rolled my eyes. "Whatever."

As we pulled in to the driveway, it was obvious both from the number of cars and the fedora-wearing hipster carrying lighting equipment toward the house that Team Prom—hair, makeup, photographer, masseuse—had arrived.

"Wish me luck," I said as Noah and I unloaded the shopping bags.

"Luck," Noah said, hugging me.

I looked up at him. "Noah?"

"Yeah?"

"Thanks for helping me today. And for not letting the fact that I used to have a crush on you weird you out or anything."

"I told you—I'm flattered that you had a crush on me. And I have a feeling that even if I decided to leave Craig for you, you're probably going to be off the market pretty soon anyway."

I snorted. "Yeah, right."

He walked toward Craig, who had pulled the Volvo he was driving in to the driveway. "I told you—prom night is magical! Stranger things have been known to happen." He shrugged.

"Oh, sweet Jesus—*finally*! Why did you not pick up your cell?" said Clarissa as I staggered through the door with the Saks bags. "Girls, get down here!" she yelled as she grabbed the bags, dumped the boxes on the floor, and $5,243.45 worth of designer shoes rolled onto the ground, much to Spencer's and Sushi's delight.

"Honey, why on earth would you get yellow?" she asked, holding up a single canary-yellow sandal.

I shrugged. "You just said to get high heels. You didn't say what color," I said as I made my way to the kitchen for a snack. It turned out that driving without a license and shoe shopping made you really hungry.

"None of them fit!" said a panicked Ashley. "Cindy! Are you *sure* these are size seven and a halfs?"

Kashi Friends for Life cereal box in hand, I rejoined them in the hallway. "It's probably the heat," I offered as I munched away. "Heat makes things—like feet—swell."

"I don't understand why those Europeans have to make everything so small," said Clarissa, sorting through the pile.

Britney tried to wiggle her foot into a pair of ivory slingbacks. "Ouch. I'm never going to be able to dance in these," she complained.

Having seen her "dance" to Jay-Z, when her bedroom door was open one day, I knew that might not have been such a bad thing for all involved.

"Me neither," said Ashley, yanking her foot out of a pair of pale pink stilettos. "I just ruined my pedicure!" she wailed.

"Maybe if you soak your feet in a tub of ice water, you can shrink them back down," I offered.

The earthshaking thumping of a bass line could be heard coming up the driveway. "We don't have time for that," said Clarissa. "The boys are here! Girls, I'll be right back—I need another Xanax."

As Clarissa remedicated herself, I did my stepsisterly duty and played shoe saleswoman by helping Britney and Ashley find shoes that wouldn't completely cut off their circulation and make their toes turn blue. Luckily for all of us (because the idea of having to drive back to Beverly Hills was terrifying), the last two pairs in the bunch worked. *Un*luckily for the Clones, they happened to be the two ugliest of the lot.

Ashley clomped, instead of glided, across the floor. "These are hideous!" she announced. She was right. They screamed "schoolmarm" instead of "sexy."

"But they *are* Prada," I pointed out. "And, you know, once you go Prada . . . you never go back."

"That's true." She sighed.

"At least yours don't have ruffles on them," moaned Britney in her frilly Vera Wangs.

Even though the Clones could be total jerks, I couldn't help but feel bad for them. Here it was, the most important night of their lives so far, and they looked like they belonged in the "Oh No They Didn't" column of a fashion magazine.

"You know, Brit, the shoe guy told me that Jessica Simpson had been in the other day and tried that *very* pair on," I said.

"Really?"

"Yup," I lied.

"Well, did she end up buying them?"

"That I don't know. But she did try them on."

"Oh." Knowing she was the proud owner of some Hollywood history made Britney stand up a little straighter. "Actually, the ruffles are kind of cute."

Clarissa ushered in Wally and Conrad, who, after taking one look at the Clones, looked like they wanted to flee into the safety of their Hummer limo and go find new dates. Due to the fact that the twins had each lost about five pounds since their original dresses had been altered, nothing fit. The material hung off the Clones, making them look like they were graduates of the Mary-Kate and Ashley School of Fashion. It was better than the Jadens, but just barely. "Okay, girls, it's photo-shoot time," Clarissa trilled. "Let's go out front!"

Having done enough good deeds to tide me over for the rest of the year, I scooped Spencer up and took him upstairs. I had no desire to play photographer's assistant and hold up fifty-pound lights, so Spencer and I watched the photo shoot from the safety of my bedroom window.

I looked over at the picture of my mom. "Tell me it's going to get better." I sighed. "Tell me that I'm not going to feel like such an alien for the rest of my life."

I watched as Clarissa waved at the limo as it sailed down the driveway. "Tell me that one day I'll meet a guy in the flesh instead of online who gets me like BklynBoy does and who's as cute as Adam Silver and that we won't go to a prom, but we'll go *somewhere*."

I looked over at Sushi to see if he had turned back into a medium, but he was compulsively licking his foot. Spencer babbled at me and went back to trying to pull off his shirt.

People were always saying "Don't wish your life away," but at that moment, I would've done anything to be in my thirties with my life all figured out. Because being a fifteen-and-a-half-year-old girl on prom night when you weren't going to the prom even though you didn't *want* to go to the prom kind of blew.

There was only one solution for the amount of psychic pain I was in: a John Hughes movie.

I was halfway into *Pretty in Pink* when Clarissa yelled for me to come downstairs.

"Okay, sugar, we're off to the country club," she said. "There's some Tofuroni in the fridge for Spencer, and because I knew you might be a little upset because everyone's at the prom except for you, I decided to put the no-sugar rule aside for the night and bought you some Ben & Jerry's Chunky Monkey." She patted me on the head. "You can even eat it in your bedroom if you want."

"Thanks," I said, trying to discreetly brush off the crumbs of the cookies that I had already eaten in my bedroom.

My dad gave me a hug. "Monkey Girl, I'm so proud of

you," he whispered. "You're a very special young woman," he said as he kissed me on the forehead.

"Thanks, Dad. You guys should go—I know how much Clarissa loves the auction part."

After a final coat of lipstick and an earring change, they left and I turned to my date for the evening, who, as usual, was in the process of trying to take his diaper off.

"Okay, *muchacho*, ready to get back to Molly and the Duckman?"

I took his gurgle as a yes and hoisted him on my hip. Halfway up the stairs, I heard a car horn beep. When I looked out the front window I saw India and Malcolm getting out of their hybrid limo.

They looked gorgeous. India was boho chic'd out in her ex-sari-turned-curve-hugging dress, while Malcolm had added a dash of funk to his tuxedo with the addition of a Pucci-inspired cummerbund.

"Omigod—you're *so* fabulous right now!" I exclaimed as I opened the front door. "But what are you doing here?"

"We wanted to give you a preprom hug," India said as she hobbled up the front steps in her heels.

My eyes filled with tears. "You guys are awesome." I went to hug Malcolm, but he held his hands out to stop me.

"Kiss, kiss," he said. "I don't want you to get tears on my tux. But I *do* love you. And even though I may give you grief at times, I think you're a real trailblazer and I'm very honored to call you my best friend."

A honk came from the limo. "We should go," said India as she hugged me. "Call if you need us."

"I will." I hugged back. "And call with updates if you can."

I headed back inside with a smile on my face. How could I possibly be depressed with friends like that?

When Spencer and I got upstairs, there was a flashing IM:

BklynBoy: so how bout I pick u up @7?
AntiPrincess: ?
BklynBoy: we DO have plans, right?
AntiPrincess: um, hello. u live in bklyn!
BklynBoy: actually . . . i don't. i live in nichols canyon.

I stared at the screen. Nichols Canyon was about two and a half miles away from Hancock Park.

AntiPrincess: what. r. u. TALKING ABOUT?????
BklynBoy: BTW—i never said I lived in bklyn. i was born there, and we lived there until I was 4. but then we moved here.
AntiPrincess: k—i'm officially freaking out. do i know u?
BklynBoy: yeah—my real name's adam.

chapter fourteen

The scream that came out of my mouth when I realized that BklynBoy was really Adam Silver was so loud that I'm sure it could be heard in China. Unfortunately, during my cramming session that day at the library, I hadn't come across anything with a title close to *What to Do When You Discover That the Guy Who's Your Cyber Best Friend Turns Out to Also Be the Most Popular Guy in Your School on Whom You've Had a Major Crush.* And even if I had, I wouldn't have bothered to read it because never in a million years would I have thought that would end up being my story.

"*Omigodomigodomigod,*" I said over and over as I stared at the computer screen. I was clueless as to what to do. I tried to call India and Malcolm, but all I got was an "all circuits are busy please try your call again later" recording.

BklynBoy: r u still there?

This *so* wasn't happening. I looked around the room for any cameras the Clones may have hid. "Am I being Punk'd?" I yelled.

Nothing.

AntiPrincess: um, yeah. and i'd really appreciate it if you told me WHAT THE HECK IS GOING ON!!!!!!!!!!!!!!

BklynBoy: ok—remember that entry in yr blog about the caste system @ school?

AntiPrincess: yeah . . .

BklynBoy: well, i read it and the rest of ur blog. i developed a cybercrush on u . . . but then when i finally wrote u and we became e-mail friends i didn't want to tell u who i was b/c i was afraid u'd stop being so honest in yr posts . . .

AntiPrincess: but i took the blog down right after that

BklynBoy: i know, but by then u thought i lived in bklyn, & i thought it would make me seem REALLY stalkerish b/c so much time had gone by if i told u who i really was then.

For a split second the whole thing *did* strike me as weird and stalkerish. But overall I found it to be the most romantic thing I could have ever imagined. Not to mention that it was the *only* romantic thing that had ever happened to me period.

BklynBoy: u have no idea how nervous i was at the yoga studio that day.

AntiPrincess: u were nervous talking to ME?? but ur ADAM SILVER!!!

BklynBoy: that's the thing-w/u i'm not "ADAM SILVER"—i'm just me. and i was nervous cos i like u. like REALLY like u.

Oh. My. God. Adam Silver really liked me. I held on to my desk to hold me up in case I fainted.

AntiPrincess: u do?

BklynBoy: yeah. i mean ur just so different from the girls i know . . .

AntiPrincess: how so?

BklynBoy: lots of ways . . . a few weeks ago i wrote this poem called "50 things i like about cindy" which i'm trying to turn into a song with my guitar teacher.

AntiPrincess: OMG—i think that's the most romantic thing i've ever heard.

BklynBoy: want to hear part of it?

AntiPrincess: yeah

BklynBoy: okay. 1. i like that u want to move to NYC. 2. i like that u listen to music w/lyrics that don't include the word 'yo.' 3. i like that yr friends are a little weird. 4. i like that u had the guts to write that letter.

I couldn't believe this. This didn't happen in real life, only in movies. I was starring in my own Nora Ephron movie. Sort of a combination of *You've Got Mail* mixed with *When Harry Met Sally* with a little bit of *Sleepless in Seattle* thrown in.

AntiPrincess: but what made you decide to come clean now?? u didn't just find out u have cancer & have 3 months to live did u?

BklynBoy: no. as far as i know i'm totally healthy. but a few days ago i got a call from noah.

So that explained Noah's cryptic response when I told him Adam had asked someone to the prom. He wasn't clueless about relationships—he was a freaking genius!

BklynBoy: he asked what i was doing on prom nite & when i told him nothing he suggested that since u weren't doing anything either, maybe the 2 of us could do nothing together . . . & that's when i asked u to be my non-prom date . . .

AntiPrincess: OMG—he totally got us together! he's like my fairy godtutor!

BklynBoy: yeah, i guess. but i thought u hated fairy tales.

AntiPrincess: i do. i'm just saying . . .

BklynBoy: so r u still up for doing something?

AntiPrincess: TOTALLY!!!!!!!!!!!!!!!!!!!!!!

My Most Romantic Moment Ever was broken by a loud burp from Spencer, followed by some delighted gurgling.

Right. Spencer. I had forgotten about him. How difficult could it be to find a babysitter? I was sure there were tons of thirteen-year-old girls in the neighborhood who, once they heard my romantic story, would pay *me* to watch Spencer so I could go out with Adam.

AntiPrincess: can we say 8 instead of 7?

BklynBoy: sure

AntiPrincess: oh . . . where are we going?

Not like it was going to make a difference in what I wore. It was either going to be jeans, jeans, or . . . jeans.

BklynBoy: it's a surprise. hey—r u weirded out by this?

AntiPrincess: um, yeah. but it's a good weirded out. at least i think it is.

BklynBoy: see u @ 8.
AntiPrincess: bye . . . adam.

I was going on a date with Adam Silver.

I tried India and Malcolm's cells again. This time at least I got their voice mails. I had to call back a few times because I kept getting cut off, but I finally got the whole story onto India's voice mail. I turned my attention to trying to find someone to take care of Spencer, and started rifling through my closet. A crisis like this called for multi-tasking.

But all the girls on Clarissa's "Possible Sitters to Use When and If Cindy Ella Has Plans" list laughed at me—even when I told them the BklynBoy/Adam Silver saga. It turned out that they had been booked months in advance—at triple their usual rate. Even if I had found someone, I would've had to cash in one of my bat mitzvah bonds to pay her. To make matters worse, I didn't own a single outfit worthy of a date with Adam.

I was doomed. Not only was I was babysitter-less and outfit-less, but I didn't have time to Google "what to talk about on a first date—even if you've already been best friends with the guy for a year and he knows everything about you."

I climbed out from under the mountain formerly known as the contents of my closet. "Are You there, God? It's me, Cindy," I demanded to the ceiling.

Nothing.

"Okay, here's the deal: if You exist, You reallyreallyreally need to help me out here."

Still nothing.

"Okay, then—I guess I'll have to check 'Atheist' anytime they ask me my religion on a questionnaire," I threatened.

More silence. Apparently God didn't care. "Thanks a lot," I said.

Who was I kidding? Maybe I could get away with passing as normal online, and maybe Adam Silver may have *thought* he liked me, but once he talked to me in person for more than a half hour (assuming I could manage to string a sentence together without stuttering), he'd see that not only were my friends weird, but that *I* was weird, too.

I needed some serious help—and my weird friends were off eating salmon and dancing to bad eighties music. I could call Phoo, but he'd just tell me to stay in the moment and breathe.

"Okay, God—I'm giving You one last chance here."

Then it dawned on me. How could I be so dense? Obviously my dislike of fairy tales was really deep.

I picked up the phone and dialed. "Noah? It's Cindy," I said when he picked up. "I know you and Craig have a prom to go to, but seeing that you seem to be my fairy godtutor, I think it's only fair that you guys get your butts over here and help me get ready for my date with Adam. Because even though I may not be going to a ball or anything, I still need to look halfway decent."

Twenty minutes later, the two of them were at my house, looking absolutely sizzling in their matching tuxes. As they weeded through my wardrobe, I dialed every woman on Clarissa's list of "Housekeepers Who Aren't Very Good at Cleaning but Seem to Like Children," but even *they* were busy.

Craig sat down on the chaise and sighed. "Well, it's official."

"What?" I asked.

"You don't have anything to wear."

"Tell me again why I can't wear jeans?"

"Because," said Noah as he rifled through my drawers, "even if you're not going to the prom, you still have a prom-night date and therefore you might want to shake it up a bit. Are you telling me you don't own *one* dress?"

I thought about it. "My bat mitzvah one."

"Let's see it," ordered Craig.

I dug it out of the far corner of my closet, next to a fuzzy robe covered with bunnies that my great-aunt Jo had gotten me for Christmukah when I was twelve. They didn't even have to say anything. Even though the dress was only two years old, it was beyond dated—complete with bedazzling. "Okay, moving on," I said as I threw the dress on the floor next to Spencer.

"Where are we going to find you a dress at seven o'clock on a Friday night?" said Noah.

I thought about it. "Well . . . there *is* one place I can think of."

I picked up Spencer and tucked him under my arm like a French baguette and we ran to Noah's car. We were on a mission.

Fifteen minutes later Spencer was gnawing on a strand of fake pearls while Noah and Craig oohed and aahed over the soon-to-be-mine red Prodo minidress at Loehmann's.

"You're going to look *stunning*," said Noah as we waited for the saleslady to ring it up with Clarissa's Amex card that I had conveniently forgotten to give back.

I looked at my watch. It was 7:20. "I'll settle for dressed."

Proving that miracles do happen, by 7:50, with Craig's help (he had seen every episode of *Queer Eye for the Straight Guy* since the pilot) and the contents of Clarissa's bathroom, not only was I dressed, but I had been brushed, straightened, scrubbed, lotioned, and perfumed into near perfection. Well, as perfect as I was going to get with only fifteen minutes to get ready and a two-minute shower.

When I came downstairs in my dress, the two of them beamed at me like proud gay uncles.

"You look like a . . . " Noah said as he zipped me up.

"Hottie?" I suggested hopefully.

"I was going to say a Bavarian countess. And everyone knows that Bavarian countesses are hot." He winked.

Even though I knew there wasn't any hope for us, I couldn't help blushing. "Thanks, guys. For everything."

Craig was busy going through the thirteen pairs of heels that didn't make the cut earlier in the day. "How about these?" he asked, holding up a pair of sexy criss-cross strapped stilettos.

"Wait a second—no one said I'd have to wear *heels*!" I began to panic. Wearing the dress was enough of a shock to my system—but having to balance on toothpicks for the evening? That was a heart attack waiting to happen. Or at least an anxiety one.

"What *do* you think you're going to wear?" asked Noah. "Flip-flops?"

I shrugged. "Why not? They're simple, yet elegant."

Craig looked like he was going to cry. "You're *not* wearing flip-flops with that gorgeous dress, even if it *is* only a knockoff."

"Fine." I sighed, rooting around in the pile of silk, satin, and leather. I settled on the lowest heel I could find: a pair of black satin Manolo Blahnik pumps.

"Happy?" I asked as I teetered my way across the room. I almost made it all the way, but at the last moment I tripped. Thankfully Craig caught me before I wiped out.

Maybe it was the panicked looks on their faces, but I started to get the feeling their faith in my ability to get through the date without hurting myself or Adam was slipping.

"I should probably try that again, huh?"

They nodded.

After a few more practice runs, not only did I start to get the hang of it, but I found the way that the heels made my butt wiggle kind of cool. Who knew being a hottie could be so fun?

Noah looked at the clock and, reaching for Craig's hand, stood up. "Well, it's five of eight, so we should get going. I don't think Adam needs to know you had a little help getting ready."

A "little" help. Talk about an understatement.

"You'll be fine," promised Craig as they walked downstairs. Reality crashed down—Adam Silver was going to be at my house in five minutes and I was going to be forced to make conversation with him for at least a couple of hours.

"Wait—you're going to *leave*?! Can't you just . . . come with me?" I threw myself in front of the door. "I think I'm going to throw up," I announced.

"You're not going to throw up," said Noah. "But if, you know, for whatever reason, things get weird, you have my cell."

"You think it's going to get weird?!" I cried. What did I get myself into?

Craig picked me up and moved me out of the way. "Why would you say something like that?" he chided Noah. "Can't you see she's already terrified?"

So much for hiding my true feelings.

He gave me one last hug and hair touch-up. "Don't listen to him. You're going to be *fine*."

Noah hugged me, too. "Yeah, I have a feeling you probably will. Call us tomorrow with a full report, okay?"

I nodded. "Okay. That is, if I don't die from humiliation first."

I had just enough time to change Spencer's diaper (I probably should have done that before putting on the dress) before the doorbell rang. With him on my hip, I ran (as much as it was possible to do that in heels) into my bedroom.

"Wish me luck," I said to the picture of my mom. Over in the corner, Sushi gave one of his happy groans. I took a deep breath and limped downstairs.

Prodo red minidress: $99.99

Manolo Blahnik shoes: $450

Look on Adam Silver's face when I answered the door: Priceless

"Wow," he finally said, with a goofy smile on his face.

"Wow," I replied with one of my own. He may have only been wearing jeans and a Neil Young T-shirt, but he was as gorgeous as ever. But something was different. Suddenly Adam Silver wasn't Adam-Silver-Biggest-Hottie-on-Campus anymore. And he wasn't the

250

nameless, faceless BklynBoy who may have been the victim of an industrial accident for all I knew, either. He was just . . . Adam. And he was already one of my best friends.

"I think I'm a little overdressed," I said, glancing down at my dress.

He shrugged. "Maybe. But there's no way I'm letting you change. You look . . . "

Jaw-droppingly beautiful? As stunning as a priceless piece of art? Exquisite to the point where there were no words to describe it?

". . . totally hot," he said.

That worked, too.

"So are you ready to go?" he asked, the goofy smile still intact.

"Yeah. But there's a slight problem: I couldn't find a babysitter, so Spencer has to come with us."

He shrugged. "That's cool. I think he'll like where we're going. But, uh, he's going to keep that on, right?"

I looked down to see that Spencer had unhooked his overalls and was headed for his diaper again.

"Yes. I promise," I said as I rehooked him. Let me just get his diaper bag."

I grabbed the bag and loaded it up with enough toys to keep Spencer busy for the next year. I also threw in my flip-flops just in case my feet went into cardiac arrest, and ran back to Adam.

"Okay. We're all set," I panted. Even though I had managed to wait fifteen and a half years for this evening, I didn't want to miss a minute now that it had arrived.

The goofy smile returned to Adam's face. Who knew that even *he* could look like a dork at times?

"What an awesome place for a date," I said as I rolled yet another skee ball into the fifty-points hole, beating Adam for the third straight game in a row. Seeing that no one else at the Santa Monica Pier arcade was wearing a designer knockoff minidress and designer heels, for the first time in my life I may have actually been the best-dressed girl in the room.

"I thought it would be a little more interesting than a movie," Adam said.

I turned to him. "No movie could've come close to this," I said shyly. "Not even if written and directed by John Hughes himself."

He walked over to me and leaned in close. "You have—"

Omigod—was I about to be kissed? Was my breath okay? Had I remembered to put on deodorant?

"A piece of cheese from the pizza right here," he said as he brushed a glob off my cheek.

Why should that night have been different from any other? At least I hadn't spilled anything on my dress. Yet.

He was so close I thought I was going to pass out. "Thanks," I whispered.

Just then we heard a huge burp and we both looked down to see Spencer sitting in his stroller, trying to shove as much cotton candy as he could into his mouth.

"Are you sure it's okay for him to be eating so much junk food?" Adam asked. In addition to the cotton candy, he had already had a cherry Sno-Kone and half of Adam's caramel apple, both of which could be found on his overalls.

"Sure. It's a special occasion," I said. "Plus it'll make him sleep really well tonight. Hey, you want to go play that game where you use the water pistol to fill the clown's mouth?"

"Okay. But you have to promise to go easy on me," he said. "So far you've beaten me at everything, which is why I think we need to do a two-out-of-three situation."

"Done," I said as I took a hunk of Spencer's cotton candy and shoved it in my mouth, not caring if I looked unladylike. It turned out that being out on a date with your best friend/crush made you really hungry. Not only that, but it was so . . . *easy*. My feet may have been killing me, but the rest of me was more comfortable than I had ever been before. That night I understood what people meant when they said you just "knew" when something was right.

Our two-out-of-three games with the clown turned into five-out-of-seven so that Adam could try and make a comeback.

"Yes!" I screamed as I won for a fifth time straight. I don't know what was going on, but there really *was* something magical in the air. Usually I sucked at anything that required coordination.

A few minutes later I was debating whether to use my winnings to get Adam a green alligator or a purple monkey.

"Hey," I heard him say.

I looked up to see Adam standing over at the railing overlooking the ocean. With the full moon shining down on him, it looked like one of those cool black-and-white photographs you see on a calendar. "Yeah?" I said.

"Come here for a sec."

I tried to stop my hands from shaking as I pushed Spencer's stroller over toward him. *Oh God,* I thought to myself. *This is going to be the Moment Where We Kiss—I just know it.*

Once I got there, he took my hand and pointed it. "Check out that sneaker floating over there," he said. "Dude, that seaweed looks *beyond* gnarly."

"How . . . *interesting*," I replied, trying not to sound too disappointed. That wasn't romantic . . . that was just plain old gross.

He put his hands on my shoulders and turned me toward him. "Cindy?"

Okay, *now* it was time for The Kiss. "Yeah?" I whispered.

My phone rang. As I dug it out of my bag, I saw Malcolm's name flash across the screen.

I clicked it on. "Malcolm, I'll call you back," I said, and clicked it off.

I took a deep breath to get back into the moment.

The phone rang again. "Seriously, I really need to call you back, Malcolm. This is *not* a good time to talk," I said before hanging up on him again. I turned back to Adam. "Sorry—you were saying." I smiled.

His hand reached toward my face. "I was just going to say . . . you've got—"

I was afraid I was going to pass out if I held my breath much longer.

"Some chili on your cheek from the chili dog," he said as he picked it off.

"Thanks." I exhaled and started rubbing at my face to remove whatever else might have been there.

"Want to go play some hoops? You have to give me a chance to win at *something*," he said.

"Sure." I sighed. I was having fun, but I was also kind of hoping we could stop with the games and get to the romantic part of the evening.

We made our way over to the basketball hoops, where, using his varsity skills, Adam finally beat me.

"Thanks," I said as he handed me a stuffed giraffe. "Want to go on the Ferris wheel?" I asked. It was obvious that if I wanted the romance, I was going to have to call on my inner nouveau feminist and take charge of the situation.

"Sure." He smiled. That smile was just amazing. It took everything in me to not whip out my phone and take a picture of it.

We climbed into the carriage, and the wheel started moving. As the carriage stopped at the top and slowly swung back and forth, the noise of the Friday-night crowd was replaced by the sound of the waves from the Pacific Ocean. It was one of those perfect moments you read about—made even more perfect when Spencer stopped babbling and drowsed off into a sugar coma, his sticky little hands clutching the giraffe's neck. I couldn't have written a better prom night.

I pointed at the sky. "Look—you can actually see some stars." Usually they were hidden behind layers of smog.

"Should we make a wish?" Adam asked.

I turned to him. "You can, but I don't need to. Not anymore."

It was then that I got my second kiss ever. But thanks to the knee-buckling, fireworks-popping chemical reaction that happened when his lips touched mine—I like to think of it as my first *real* one. Needless to say, it was worth the wait.

"Wow," I said when we came up for air. "That was amazing."

He laughed. "For someone who's a writer, that's the best you can come up with?"

"Hmm . . . I think I might need to relive the experience to come up with a better adjective."

Thankfully he was more than happy to help me out with that one.

"I'm not going to end up as the subject as one of your letters to the editor, am I?" he asked as the Ferris wheel started moving again.

"Nope. Maybe a novel, though."

Back down on the ground, we continued our lip-lock workout as we pushed a passed-out Spencer through the crowd.

"Hey, is that your phone?" I heard Adam say at one point.

"Hmm?"

"Your phone."

I rifled through the diaper bag. "Oh. Yeah."

I was all ready to yell at Malcolm again when I saw *Dad* flashing across the screen.

"Omigod," I panicked. "It's my dad. Um, hello?" I said, praying that he wouldn't be able to hear the organ music.

"Hi, honey. Just wanted to see how you were holding up."

"Oh. I'm fine. Um, just watching a documentary about the history of amusement parks on the Discovery Channel."

"Good. Clarissa was worried that you might have fallen into a depression or something because of the prom thing. She said there was some TV movie about a girl who OD'd because she didn't go."

"Nope. I'm fine." I smiled as I watched Spencer snuggle up to the giraffe. "It actually turned out to be a much better night than I thought it would be."

"Okay. Well, we should be home in about a half hour or so."

I looked down at my watch—it was already eleven-thirty. Not only had I snuck out of the house—but I had snuck out of the house with a one-year-old and tranquilized him with cotton candy. I figured I was looking at about two to three years of solitary confinement in my bedroom.

"Okay. See you then. If I'm not sleeping already, that is." I clicked the phone closed and shoved Adam toward the exit. "We've got exactly a half hour to get me home." As we ran down the boardwalk to the car, with Spencer in his stroller, my heel caught between the wood planks. As much as I tried to yank my foot free, it wouldn't budge.

"Hey! I'm stuck," I yelled to Adam, who was a good ten feet ahead.

He came running back to my side. "What happened?"

"The heel got caught," I said. By this time I had gotten my foot out of the shoe and was on my hands and knees trying to wriggle the heel out of the plank.

"Here—let me help you," he said, kneeling down.

The two of us wiggled away, but the sucker was jammed in tighter than a Clone in a pair of Rock & Republic jeans. Suddenly I heard a snap and I went flying back onto my butt. I looked down at my hand and saw that my Manolo Blahnik high heel had become a flat. I looked at Adam, who looked at me.

"Whoops," the two of us said in unison before cracking up.

"Can you believe these things cost four hundred and fifty dollars and they just break like that? What a rip-off," I said. I began rummaging through Spencer's diaper bag and pulled out my flip-flops. "Whereas *these* cost only eight, *thankyouverymuch* J.Crew Spring Sale." I stood up and slid them on, wiggling my toes to try to get some feeling back into them. I shoved the Manolos in the bag. "Okay. Much better," I said as we took off again.

How we got all the way from Santa Monica to Hancock Park in twenty minutes when the prom limo logjam was worse than a Mafia funeral remains a mystery. But, then again, the entire night had been filled with miracles, and magic, and all that good stuff I had read about in books but never in a million years thought could happen to me.

"So . . . you want to do something tomorrow?" Adam asked me after our fifth "just one more good-bye kiss" on my doorstep.

"Okay."

"And how 'bout Sunday after you get off work?"

"Sure."

"And I was thinking maybe Monday night, if you're not busy, you might want to go to the Dodger game with me."

"Definitely."

Was I just dreaming it, or did Adam Silver seem to want to spend every waking moment with me? Not that I was complaining or anything. I went ahead and pinched my arm, just in case.

"What are you doing?" he asked.

"Pinching myself to see if this is really happening," I replied.

"I have a better way for you to tell," he said.

"How?"

"With this," he said as he kissed me again.

That worked for me.

After one last kiss, I flip-flopped my way inside, and, after putting Spencer to bed, floated into my own room, where the smile on my face remained for the entire night.

epilogue

I woke up at seven the next morning and saw the grinning giraffe smiling up at me from the floor. I smiled back. Apparently the night before really *had* happened, which was a good thing because finding out I had dreamed the whole thing would have sucked big-time.

Normally I would've waited until the reasonable hour of eight to wake up India and Malcolm, but I owed Malcolm several calls. Plus, becoming boyfriend/girlfriend with Adam Silver was the most special occasion I could imagine, so I dialed away.

As soon as I was able to conference India and Malcolm in, the two of them took turns shrieking into the phone and chanting "OMIGODOMIGODOMIGOD." I filled them in on the entire story—from IM session to last kiss of the night. Malcolm was so shocked he didn't interrupt once. It turned out that my night had been a lot more exciting than theirs. According to Malcolm, the prom was about as much fun as watching reruns. Unfortunately Colin spent the entire evening outside trying to get reception on his Sidekick so he could e-mail some guy from Miami he had met the weekend before on MySpace, while Jackson spent the whole time trying to convince Maya Mornell's best friend, Staci Wenner, that, really, it was her and not Maya that he had always liked and that they should get a room at the hotel and hang out after the prom was over.

"And *then* to make the evening even worse, the air-conditioning broke. Do you have any *idea* how disgusting a room full of guys who have just finished dancing to Justin Timberlake smells?" Malcolm asked.

"What about the Clones?" I asked. There was no way I wanted to actually hear about the prom from the twins.

"You mean the winners of the 'Worst Dressed' award of the evening?" Malcolm asked. "The last I heard Britney refused to come out of the bathroom because her dress ripped as she was shaking her booty to Beyoncé and the entire prom got to see firsthand that she wasn't wearing any underwear."

"Hopefully someone filmed it and it'll be up online soon?" I asked.

"Cin, you're so lucky you didn't go," said India. "It was such a waste of time. There's no way I'm ever going to another prom in my life. I'd rather stay home and be force-fed steak by terrorists. Believe me—I much rather would've had your night. How cool is it that you're in love now?! I'm so excited for you!"

"*Everyone* at that prom would've rather had her night," said Malcolm.

"See what happens when you're true to yourself?" said India. "I totally think you should write about this and see if some magazine will print it."

Hmm. Maybe I would write about it at some point, but between hanging out with Adam and savoring every postkiss activity ("This is the first shower I've ever taken since I kissed Adam," "This is the first bowl of cereal I've had since I kissed Adam"), my schedule was already pretty full.

But the best moment of all happened on Monday morning, right before lunch, when the halls were full of kids gossiping about how people decided to write in Alice Kim, president of the Science Club, on the Prom Queen ballot in protest and she won in a landslide.

I was at my locker thinking that this was the first time I had dropped a book on my foot postkiss, when there was a tap on my shoulder. As I turned around, my boyfriend—a.k.a. Adam Silver—was standing there holding my broken-heeled Manolo Blahnik.

"I found this in the backseat of my car this morning," he said with a smile. "It must've fallen out of Spencer's bag."

"Thanks." I smiled back as I took it from him.

"By the way, I like you much better in flip-flops," he whispered, right before he leaned in and kissed me.

"Me, too," I said. You'd think that after a weekend of kissing, I would have been used to it, but each kiss still left me feeling like I had been electrocuted. In a good way.

I turned around and was greeted by the open-mouthed stares of the entire Castle Heights student body—the widest of which belonged to the Clones.

I shut my locker, and Adam and I headed outside to join Malcolm and India under our tree. I was yet again the topic of most of the conversations taking place at school.

However, this time I wasn't complaining.

My classmates may have gotten crystal champagne flutes engraved with *Castle Heights High School Senior Prom* that Friday night, but I had gotten something a hundred times better: a guy who, if the last seventy-two hours were any indication, totally adored me as much as I adored him.